DIALOGUES
WITH THE
DEVIL

DIALOGUES WITH THE DEVIL

By Taylor Caldwell

A FAWCETT CREST BOOK

Fawcett Publications, Inc., Greenwich, Conn.
Member of American Book Publishers Council, Inc.

FOREWORD

This is not a theological book, though it adheres to the Judeo-Christian traditions and to Holy Scripture, and to the traditions and tales of ancient as well as modern religions. It began in a lighthearted mood—in order to give Lucifer his day in court—and then it stopped being lighthearted and became very somber and grim indeed, as Lucifer presented his case against mankind, and the problem of Good and Evil, and its mystery. If I were superstitious, which I am, of course, I should say that two personalities took over the book in midpassage, but what they are I do not know. Certainly the thoughts in the book are not my thoughts!

In the Judeo-Christian tradition Luciel, the Dayster, the angel of light, is named Lucifer. The ancient Persians called him Ahriman, the Egyptians, Apap, the old Teutons, Loki, and he was Tiamet of the Babylonians, Siva of the old and the new Hindoo religion, (or Manyu, "wrath,") and Beelzebub of the Chaldeans, and Pluto, the god of The Underworld, of the Greeks and Romans. In all traditions he fell from Heaven because of the sin of pride and disobedience and rebellion, and became the slave and master of men, tempting them to eternal death and perdition. He has as many names as God, in dead and living religions, but, like God, his nature never changes, nor his objectives.

Through all traditions the idea of Lucifer's ultimate redemption runs steadily, though in Christian theology that tradition was denounced as a heresy in the fifth century A.D. Nevertheless, it persists. The ancient traditions entertain the possibility of the eventual remorse of the spirit of Evil and its reconciliation with God. Who is to say?

In the Book of Job Lucifer always presents himself before the Lord as "one of the sons of God," and implies that he is not God's enemy but man's, and that he is the prosecutor of man before God, the witness to his crimes, the denouncer who demands the extreme punishment of eternal death for the blasphemy of man's existence. Man's little imagination has presented him in horrific apparitions, some of them absurd and jejune, horned and hoofed, yet he was the greatest, most powerful and most resplendent of the archangels and is still an archangel. To denigrate him as a ridiculous figure, and ugly and paltry, is wrong, and does a disservice to God Who can create nothing ugly—only man can do that—and in the belittling of Lucifer there is a great danger. Evil is nothing to belittle, nor the anguish of Evil. Lucifer, as the Holy Bible states, is Prince of this World, and certainly he cannot be as hideous as the other self-proclaimed "princes" we have seen in this century, and in past centuries. And his power is only a little less than the power of the Almighty, and has its expression only in Man.

I have discovered that men are always fascinated by the thought of Lucifer, perhaps because evil is always more dramatic than good, more spectacular, more bloody, and more frightful, and when men are not comedians—though they never seem aware of the comedy of their being—they are, at heart, dramatists and tragedians. Yet, strangely, the tragedy of the Sacrifice on the Cross does not touch them greatly, and therein is another mystery.

Though many philosophers, historians, and some geologists deny that there were any other continents on this earth, Terra, besides the ones we know, the Encyclopedia Britannica says in its 1943 edition: "In Devonian times Africa was already an ancient continent, but lay far south of its present position and extended into the Antarctic. A second continent stretched across northern Europe to the northeast of North America. Between them lay the ocean geologists call Tethys. In the Western Hemisphere narrow seas existed, in the east and west of what is now North America, and low land, submerged later, lay between. In the old red sandstone are the first well-preserved remains of vertebrates comprising many strange types."

So despite ridiculing remarks about the ancient lost continents of Atlantis and Mu, and others, there does seem considerable proof that these sunken continents did exist, as Lucifer remarks in his book, and they went their way in water as we will go our way in fire, as St. John prophesied. But this time the world as we know it will not survive.

In these final nights before the Apocalypse—mentioned in Matthew 24 and in other books in the Holy Bible—let us pray, before it is too late:

"Agnus Dei, Who take away the sins of the world—
Have mercy on us!"

Taylor Caldwell

DIALOGUES
WITH THE
DEVIL

SALUTATIONS

to the Lord God of Hosts, the Father Almighty, Creator of Heaven and worlds and suns, the Holy of Holies, the Ineffable One, the Serenity of Universes, the Splendor of Life, the Progenitor of archangels, angels, cherubim and seraphim, Powers and Dominions, Princes and Principalities, the Triune God, the Perpetrator of men—and my Father.

I wish to assure you, my Father, that it has given me no unsurpassed pleasure that Melina, one of the sons of Arcturus, has now become a wasteland, devoid of the curse of human life, and moves about his parent sun in glorious silence, except for the winds which blow from pole to pole. Nothing sentient survives. The seas move in and out unseen by human or animal eye. I regret the innocent animals, but am I guilty of the men of Melina? No, it was Your Majesty who created them, despite my warnings—as I warned You from the beginning of time.

This morning, while I stood on the black sands of Uturia, the great sea, I meditated on the blessed silences where men are not. I saw the blue-white light of the tremendous Arcturus lifting over the green waters, and felt his first hot kiss on my cheek. I knew that within these waters lived no fish or serpent any longer, no sinless fin, no wild and uncorrupted eye. That was my sadness, my only sadness. Did I destroy Melina, and leave her mighty white cities uninhabited, her tangle of vast roads pale only with dust? Did I condemn her red fields and meadows to give fruit no longer, and offer nourishment never again to a blue tree? I am guiltless of this. I do not force men; I suggest and tempt. It is their will that they obey me, that they offer me their deepest adoration and most passionate allegiance, and that they turn, always, from You. I do not exploit their wickedness; they choose it for themselves. I merely give them the opportunity to pursue evil to its ultimate. The horizons of Melina are now without meaning, for Death has no meaning, as You, my Father, and I know only too well. You have said it often, in all Your worlds, in the tongues of all creation—but men do not believe You. They believe only me.

The continents of Melina know no voice, no, not the voice of man, or bird or beast. I flew over them all. Nothing survives. Did I do this thing alone? I did not do it at all! Man did it. Ah, the deadly exaltation of evil, the furious energy, the enthusiasm, the tireless striving, the fierce joy, the sleepless passion! I know them well, for it was I who created them and gave them as my hellish gift to mankind in all Your boundless worlds and rainbowed universes. What has virtue to offer in comparison, though virtue is eternal life? Does virtue possess the drama, the violence, the color, the frantic vehemence, the terrible euphoria, the laughter and noise and ecstasies of evil, and yes, the enormous capacity for destruction? Verily, it does not. It is a weariness to man, as You have regretfully observed ten thousand times ten thousand millennia over and over. The desire for wickedness and death is far greater in the breasts of mankind than the desire for innocence and life.

Eight billion souls from Melina now occupy my domain, and I loathe them, for all their proffered and frenzied worship. (They do not repent—yet, but the time will come!) To You, my Father, there rose only six thousand souls who had resisted me. A poor harvest! You are the Sower, but I am inevitably the Reaper, and so shall it be throughout eternity. You are the Vineyard, but it is I who harvest and press the grapes and drink the wine. You are the Tree, but I garner the fruit. You are the Meadow, but the grain fills my granaries. Do You consider that I rejoice in this? I do, only to the extent that I can prove that Your Majesty was wrong from the beginning. It is no joy to me to wound You, Who have so many wounds, and

Who shall receive so many countless more. But You know this. If I had tears to shed I would shed them for my Father, Who loved me, Who called me His son and His Star of the Morning. It was You Who mourned me and exclaimed, "How have you fallen!" But I have not fallen lower than man. That would be impossible.

I have been called the patron saint of scientists. Yet, I did not deliver the secret of suspending the time-space-matter continuum to the men of Melina. I merely conducted a dialogue with them, as a teacher, a suggester. It was theirs to recoil, to reject with terror and loathing. It was in their hands to destroy the formulae, in horror. But alas, they hated their brothers with so much infernal passion! It is true that I am the father of wars, the songster of hatred, but again, it is in the power of men to reject, for do they not possess free will, that frightful gift you bestowed on men and angels so long ago? But though I am the father of wars, I do not precipitate them. There is no need for my own energies to be involved in this matter of fraternal detestation, nor do I need to stimulate it. It is in the nature of man to hate his brother; he needs little encouragement. And, in the case of Melina, I gave no overt assistance. I only led his scientists along the path of ebullient speculation, and men are notable for their deathly ebullience—and the languid and ridiculing eye they cast on virtue.

Once a scientist's speculations are aroused he is anxious to apply them objectively. This did Melina's scientists do, as they have done in ten thousand worlds before. They did not think: "How will this benefit my race?" They only thought: "How can this be used to eliminate my enemies?" For man, as Your Majesty knows, cannot live unless he creates his own enemies. He finds existence dull beyond imagining if he has no foes. His pursuit from birth is not goodness and mercy and love. It is only destruction. It is his nature.

I did not even suggest to the men of Melina that they could use their inspired formulae to destroy their "enemies." They immediately leaped to the conclusion. Had no enemies remained from their last four wars, they would have raised them up again. Happily for me, sorrowfully for You, the continent of Anara still retained many millions—even after all those wars!—and the continent of Predama had six billion inhabitants. There were also the two subcontinents of Larya and Litium, teeming with men who had experienced wars but briefly. It was the scientists of Predama who discovered the secret of suspending the time-space-mass continuum, and who lusted to experiment with it. Unfortunately for them, I misled them into believing that they had also discovered the method of limiting the effect of suspension to their "enemies." They were certain that they held the terrors of the universe in their clay-molded hands! It was my little jest that I assured them that they were immune from the hell they finally decided to unloose. My little jest. Still, I am guiltless. They could, until the final awful moment, have withdrawn from their decision. I used no force. They were no slaves. They were free. They chose to die. Certainly, it was not their plan to vaporize themselves together with their "foes." But evil is madness and has no pity, and therefore it is confusion thrice compounded. Evil men possess no wits. They are easily led to believe what they wish to believe, and the men of the continent of Predama believed that they would suffer no consequences from the murder of their brothers, and that the cities and the treasures of their fellows would survive.

In two moments it was done—and Melina is cursed no longer by the race of men. Alas, that You manifested Yourself to them one thousand times through the ages! The generations who saw Your manifestations believed, but their children and their children's children cried—as they cry always— "It is only a myth! It did not occur! It was the dream of old men in their dotage, or the fancier of tales in the light of our three moons, or the desire of those who face the darkness of extinction of the morrow. It is only a vision of what is Not Possible, for there is only reality, and man is reality, and what is seen and felt and smelled and tasted and heard with our senses is the only objectivity, and only truth. We are too Advanced for myths; we have achieved maturity and wisdom and intellect. Begone with Myths! They are the lumber of dead yesterdays, the rubble of a primitive people, the legends of our racial childhood. There is only Today, and we are that Day. There is but one God, and His Name is Mankind, and science is His prophet."

Alas, alas—for You my Father. The men of Melina live no more. Shall You raise up another race? Be certain if You do that I shall tempt them to their certain death —which will be their own choice and not mine.

Your son, Lucifer

GREETINGS

to Lucifer, the Infernal of infernals, the Fallen One, the Majesty of ten million hells, the Dark Shadow, the Emperor of demons, the Lost Archangel, the Destroyer, the Adversary of all that lives, the Seducer of souls, the father of despair, the Murderer of Hope, the Evil of Evils, the Progenitor of Lies, the Inventor of fear, the Most Unfortunate:

Our Father has asked me to reply to your letter, as always He has requested this of me in the past.

As always, you fear that He will hold you in supreme guilt for the death of Melina, fourth from Arcturus, who has lost one of his sons. And again, I must assure you that He holds you, though not entirely blameless, not the ruthless executioner men consider you to be. You are, in truth, only their servant, and this Our Father knows. You are the designer, but it is men who project the design into reality. You are the whisperer, but it is men who shout your words from the rooftops and the mountains, from the valleys to the seas, of many worlds. He knows your endless sorrow, your secret desire that men will resist you, for does not your hope of Heaven depend upon man rejecting you? You are the slave, not the master, of men. You are bound to their desires like a condemned one to the wheel—and you are truly condemned. You are called the prince of a multitude of worlds, but you are the captive of your subjects. Men hail you as their god, but you are a god in chains. We who stand with the Father weep for you, and there was none like unto you, my brother, Lucifer, none so magnificent, so glorious in light, so noble of countenance, so endowed with beauty and subtlety, so puissant in word and deed, so brilliant of eye and strong of masculine voice, so fearless, so full of laughter and humor. We mourn you also, as Our Father mourns you, and each step that you approach Heaven again is hailed in the shining blue halls of Our Father's house and is heralded from the blazing battlements. Each step you fall again—through the offices of men—causes a brief darkness to pass over us. But we have spoken of this before.

When last we met together on neutral ground, you said to me, "Michael, had not Our Father given you strength you should not have hurled me from the deeps of Heaven." It is true, and this I acknowledged. But I struck you in the heart with a thunderbolt of sorrow, and that is the most terrible thunderbolt of all. It is not to be confused with repentance, for you do not repent. Repentance means penance and restitution, and these are now beyond your greatest powers, for they are withheld from you, not by your will, but by the deeds of men. Slave! Your brothers weep for you. How fearful it is to be the slave of what you despise! How full of anguish it is for a proud archangel to be dependent on the whims of those he considers to be the most abject and detestable of all the creations! It is as if a king were subject to a beast. Unlike you I know that what Our Father ordains is not to be hated and loathed, no matter how inexplicable. Are we the holders of His secrets? Do we know the future as He knows it? His Laws are our Laws, and it is our joy to be obedient to them. It was only you, and the angels with you, who revolted against the Law, holding yourself wiser than the Godhead, appalled that creatures of clay and earth, of water and wind, should share with you the prerogatives of free will, the gift of eternal life, the ecstasy of gazing on the Face of the Lord Our God and Father, the rapture of Heaven, the ultimate glimpse of the Beatific Vision. But though so many myriads of us were as troubled as yourself, my brother, we knew that Our Father has His reasons, and that we must bow to them, and obey. Are we of His Mind, though we are of His essence? Can we create Life, as He creates it? Can we lift the systems and the universes out of chaos and nothingness, and set them to

singing with the harmonies of Heaven? No, these are not
in our power. But you refused to acknowledge that Our
Father has His reasons. Your arrogance was wounded,
your anger aroused. There was always a certain precipi-
tance in your nature from the beginning. But none of us
believed that you would transgress beyond the boundary
forbidden to archangel, angel and man.

You told me that you were aghast that men would be
permitted to call God "Our Father," as we are permitted.
That was in the days before you totally transgressed,
when it was only an enraged thought in your mind. You
were jealous of His Majesty, obsessed with jealous love
for Him, fearful that in some way His Holiness might be
tarnished, His Honor brought to humiliation. You would
isolate Him from love—the love of His creatures, however little. You would hold Him only to yourself. There
were moments when others of your brothers approached
Him, even myself, and your eye sparkled wrathfully, and
your hand lay on the hilt of your sword. Your mouth
opened to protest, though then you swallowed your rage,
and even smiled as if at yourself and your presumption.
You would never have revolted had not man been
molded from the dust, and if he had not parted his lips
and had not said "Lord!" as we say the Word.

Our Father, Who knows all the thoughts of angels and
men, and all their deeds, was troubled by you from the
beginning. Did He know that you would transgress beyond the boundary that must not be crossed, which is the
greatest of sins? We shall never know. Love can destroy
as well as evil, and if you were cast from Heaven it was
not because of your evil but through your haughty love.
We who are your brothers know this too well. But we
have spoken of this together, you and I, through all the
eons, whenever we have met. When we have encountered
each other on the dark way of death, over which I conduct the multitudes of souls which have been saved, I
have looked upon your gloomy countenance and your un-
readable eyes with regret and sadness. At those times you
have moved aside, and have not attempted to hinder me.
But these were the souls which had rejected you. Was

your gloom a pretense? We pray it is so. For each soul that enters into Heaven is a step upward for you; each soul that descends with you plunges you deeper into the pit of your own creation. How you must hate that soul!

You have asked of Our Father if He will create a new race on Melina. He will not give you that answer.

But mourn with Him that you succeeded in your encouragement of the evil that dwelt in the hearts of the men of Melina! The death of that planet was another great death for you. Do not taunt the Lord, for you taunt only yourself, and this you know, alas, only too well. True it is that Our Father grieves for Melina, but He grieves also for you.

Is there no way to appeal to your pity, though you have vowed that you will have no pity towards men? Consider again Terra, third from a certain star (a dwarf yellow sun, that little guardian of nine infinitesimal worlds, that feeble dim spark in the mighty Galaxy which I rule, a Galaxy of enormous suns, too many even for my own counting, and whose numbers are known only to God). Why, of all the billions of planets in Creation did God choose to be born of Terra, a hesitant, trembling flash of blue, a darkling little spot, an unseen tiny glimmer in a whirlwind of planets, whose name is not known to the children of mighty distant worlds in other universes? You have asked that with wrath and fury, many thousands of times. I have no answer for you. Our Father made Terra's soil sacred with His Holy Blood, which He shed for that world, and for all its souls. We have never understood, for this He has not done before. He chose the smallest and the weakest, the frailest and meanest, the most insignificant, the most obscure and shrouded, the most crepuscular, the most hidden, the most tremulous, the most unsound and uncertain, the most fragile and coldest, the least endowed with the reflected beauty of Heaven. On this barren and ignominious spot He laid down His human life in agony, and it astounded not only you, but your brothers also. You alone questioned, and turned away in disgust, and then your anger was aroused beyond what it had ever been aroused before. You have tempted uncountable worlds to their death in the past, but never were you so affronted before by any world, and never did you vow so pitilessly to destroy it. Its creatures were no match for you, Lucifer, yet you have no pity.

This fledgling world has been redeemed by God. Have other worlds been redeemed also by that awesome Redemption? This is known only to Our Father. He lifted the feeblest in His Hands and that must have been for the most regal reason, for He pressed it to His Breast. But did He not say, "The first shall be last, and the last first"? Terra is, above all worlds, the most humble. Yet, He redeemed it, and perhaps in that Redemption the shadow of evil was lightened on other worlds also, and death driven away.

But there are so many myriads of worlds where your dark wings have not fallen, and whose children know the Face of God and obey His laws! Are these beyond your temptation? We hope, for your sake, my brother, that this is so.

Have pity on Terra. So poor a little world for your mighty efforts! So small an arena for your powers! Alas, however, pride dwells there, and hatred also, and these draw your attention. He died in His human flesh for her, and we know that this you cannot forgive. Yet, have pity.

Your brother, Michael

GREETINGS

to my brother, Michael, Archangel of the Conformists who ask no troubling questions:

Always have I loved you, dear brother, despite your simplicity! I see again, as I write you now, your shining blue eyes, your golden hair, your tall and muscular body, your heroic arms, your sudden smile, your strong hands, your firm feet, and your broad shoulders. Do not think I mock you with these words. I write them with admiration. I always loved your conversation, though it was not notable for challenging speculation and was often too grave. Yet you are often merry, and your laughter boomed through Heaven. But, you are too simple.

For another time without count you have asked me to have some pity on Terra, that miserable speck of congealed slime that lumbers heavily about a wretched dwarf yellow star in a forgotten boundary of your own Galaxy. There have been moments when I have considered if Our Father had not deliberately tormented me by choosing that depraved little morsel for the scene of His universal Redemption. From among the inconceivable bounty of His billions of worlds He chose the most loathsome and insignificant, the dullest and most lightless, the most stupid and degenerate. Is there a meaning in that? Who knows His Mind? You, too, have asked that question. I, therefore, am not alone. You, however, accept meekly. But I am not meek and so there can never be any acceptance in me, but only incredulity and affront. Endless other worlds have sinned and fallen, under my tutelage and suggestion, beautiful vast worlds of blinding color and enormous vistas and splendid cities, and with men who could at least claim to have a wink of intelligence. But He did not choose one of them. He chose the most vulgar, the most animalistic, the muddiest, the dirtiest, the most inarticulate, the least endowed with poetry and comprehension, without mercy and faith and learning. It is not worthy even to be called a latrine or a gutter, this murderer of prophets and heroes, this murderer of God, Himself. This delighter in filth, in sins most abominable and unspeakable, this arrogant little squeak in the song of creation! I have felt some pity for other worlds which have fallen, for they had some splendor and some glory. But for Terra I have only revulsion. Half desert, half storm, half-polluted seas, half-eroded mountains, it is a fit habitation of the creature which reared itself on its hind legs and dared to call itself a man!

You, too, were present with a host of my unfallen brothers, when God was killed by the animal who pretends to be human. (Dear Heaven, so base a beast!) Do you remember that day, Michael? Ah, you can never forget! Nor can I.

You will say, as you have said before, that it was Our Father's will, and that His son was born for that very purpose of the one creature unstained by the contemptible sins of her fellowman. It was a Consummation, you have told me, that He designed from the beginning of time. But the Consummation was man's doing, his unpardonable sin. (You do not agree with me in this, though you have no other explanation. You will say that I am incapable of understanding, but I was always wiser than you, beloved brother.)

Would other worlds have consummated that supreme crime, other worlds fallen and now vanished? I think not. They, evil though they were, would have revolted against such a Consummation, even if they had considered the Christ only a man as they were men. They were not forever intent on the murder of the innocent, for the destruction of the harmless, despite their tedious wars. The manifestly pure and good never aroused their hatred, as the men of Terra are endlessly aroused. Even if the good angered them they recognized its virtue, and though they often exiled it, out of expediency and because it was troublous and interfered with the enjoyment of life, they did not torture and condemn it to death in a most infamous way. They even gave it an amused honor, though they did not wish to embrace it. They had tolerance, so they were truly men, suffering what was incomprehensible and annoying. But the men of Terra are not really men, though you would deny this. Does Our Father realize that in truth the creatures of Terra are not absolute men, and was it His desire that He raise them to manhood? If so, He has dolorously failed. Those who are men on Terra can be counted only in the thousands, and it was always so. They conceal themselves with justified terror and prudence from those who presume to call themselves their fellows. They hide in far places, behind walls and in jungles, in the lost sanctuaries and in the deserts. When they emerge with words of love and mercy and compassion they are greeted with derision, or with the inevitable murder. Have they not learned? Will they never learn? The man who comes with the bread of pity and the bread of life in his hands is doomed, forever and a day, on Terra, to hatred and assassination.

Our Father, through the ages of Terra, inspired priests of all religions with the secret and mystical knowledge that He would send His Son to man to open again the gates of eternal life, which you, yourself, were bidden to close to him. There was not a religion through the ages which did not dimly proclaim the coming of the Redeemer. The priests of Babylonia, of Egypt, of Greece, of Rome, of Persia, of wearisome other nations also, proclaimed this living Promise. (And so did the priests of the dead continents of Atlantis, Lemuria and Mu and Endria.) The prophets repeatedly announced the coming of God unto man, in his flesh. Do I need to recall to you the words of the prophet, Isaias: "Unto us a Child is born. Unto us a Son is given. The Government is upon His shoulder, and His Name shall be called Wonderful, Counselor, God the Mighty, the Father of the world to come, the Prince of Peace." His Mother was prophesied: "Who is she that looks forth as the bright morning, fair as the moon, clear as the sun, and terrible as an army with banners?" Unto the priests of Khem, in Egypt, the prophecy was given also, and they wore the Cross of infamy ages before the vile deed was consummated in Judea, and the pyramids were inscribed with the Cross, which was to mankind the sign of Resurrection and life. The Greeks had their mysterious altar to the Unknown God, and awaited Him. The Romans vaguely understood also, and in the realms beyond the seas which men did not know as yet. God did not withhold His secret, nor come in stealth without prophecy. Yet, when He came He was murdered.

It has been endlessly amusing to me to listen to men since the day of that most infamous murder. "We should not have killed Him, had He been born to us instead of the Jews," they vehemently declare. "We should have cherished Him and raised Him upon our shoulders and cried 'Hosannah to the Lord!' " Liars, liars! The men of Judea, who had witnessed through the ages the mercy of God, said to Jesus, "Had the prophets been born to us we should not have killed them!" But all men kill their prophets and their heroes. They cannot endure their proximity, their implicit reproach.

Had not God been born to the Jews His Name would still be unknown among the children of men, for It would have been obliterated. But the Jews had cherished and remembered the prophecies of the Messias, and when He came among them thousands of them indeed did cry, "Blessed is He who comes in the Name of the Lord!" It was not an accident that He chose His Apostles from among the Jews, for only they were devoted to the prophecy, and recognized Him. (But how ironical it was that Peter, who had said, "You are the Christ," denied Him three times! Is that not natural for man?) I often conjecture: Had not Israel been oppressed by Rome, and in terror of her, would the Christ have been yielded pusillanimously by the priests of Judea to the Romans? Had Israel been free, would she not have joyously lifted up her Lord and proclaimed Him to the nations? But then the prophecies of Isaias would not have been fulfilled. It is a great mystery and I despised it from the beginning. The ways of God are indeed inscrutable, and a weariness.

It was the Jews who spread the "good news" to the children of men, that the Messias had been born and had died for the salvation of men, according to the prophecies. It was the Jews who, for three hundred years, cried forth the words of deliverance from evil—from me. They took His Name to the Greeks and the Romans and the Persians and the Egyptians—and died in their own blood for the message. They died joyfully—for nothing. For I followed them everywhere, and raised up haters and cynics among the listeners, and skeptics among the wise and urbane—as I raise them to this day. I whispered, "Nonsense!" to the multitudes, and they laughed at the Jews and struck them down, as they had struck them down in Egypt and Persia and Syria and Babylonia. Yes, and other prophets in Atlantis and Lemuria and Mu and Endria, until the day Our Father sank them under the waters in the great Flood. And in Terra today, where the whisper and laughter and merriment announce, "God is dead!" It is my ultimate success.

You have asked me always, "Why do you do this thing?" I do not do it out of hatred for Our Father, Whom I love. I do it to prove to Him that He was wrong from the beginning, and that He must erase, forever, the memory of Him from among the cattle who dare to call themselves men. Shall a beast share in the feast of the Holy of Holies? It is a profanation. The trample of hoofs in the Temple must cease! The ass and the wild owl and the serpent must know the Temple no more. I shall not rest until this is accomplished. I shall not rest until Terra is dead, and dies in her own fire and blood, for she has blasphemed God too long.

I have given Terra the formula for her death, as I have given similar formulae to the men of other worlds. You will not rejoice with me that this abattoir of God and prophets and heroes will soon be caught up in the whirlwind of flame as prophesied by the prophet, Joel. But then, you do not share with me my abhorrence of mankind, wherever it has manifested itself throughout the universes.

The suns and the worlds were created for angels, and not animals who stink of manure and sweat and vice and bowels and bladders and disease and all vileness.

It is again my vow that I shall not cease until this insult against God has been purged by universal death, and until the province of the galaxies belongs to angels only. If God will not do it I shall.

Your brother, Lucifer

GREETINGS

to my brother, Lucifer, who desires, in his enigmatic heart, that he be refuted and rejected and that the Glory of God be proclaimed forever to angels and men—though he would deny it:

I have read your letter with sorrow, for I know the anguish of your spirit. I, too, remember you, and your grand appearance and the glory of your presence. How is it possible, I often ask myself, for poor men to resist you, who are so many apparitions, all of them seductive? So small a foe, man! So helpless, so feeble, so confused, so blind, so dejected, so little! I look upon him and weep. The wonder to me is not that he has often rejected and blasphemed God, but that he has remembered Him so long, despite the scorners and the philosophers and the erudite scholars. The wonder to me is not that he resists the tender blandishments of the Lord in such multitudes, but that so many men—though you would deny this— hold Him so preciously to their hearts and adore His Name daily after their death, and they turn from you as they turned from you in life, and they fly like radiant birds to the bosom of their Lord.

You would scornfully call this "simplicity." But virtue is simple and easily understood. It is only evil that is complex, complicated, twisted in all its ways, and devious. Virtue is a stream of bright water going faithfully to the sea. But evil winds through many passages and gorges and chasms, and it takes on many intricate colors and hides itself in alien caverns. Evil has a thousand conversations and uncountable perverse rituals. It is a thousand undisciplined wheels within a wheel, all zealously spinning. Life, on the contrary, is direct and without guile, and has no arguments, for Life *is,* and there can be no argument in the presence of order. Evil lives in a multitude of philosophies and controversies and conjectures and speculations. It attempts, always, to argue Life out of existence, and is triumphant only where there is nothingness. In short, it is death.

There is, in evil men, the will to die, to be absolved from the burden of being, to be rescued from seeking an answer—though the answer is so plain and so unequivocal. Evil seeks absolution from the necessity to accept. It shares one thing in common with virtue—the desire for adherents. Man cannot live alone, either in virtue or in evil. As virtue cannot tolerate the evil, neither can the vile tolerate the just. One must perish. You will say that evil is always victorious. No, not always, for does Life not endure? Life cannot exist in the presence of death and midnight cannot be while the suns shine.

The poor men on Terra shout passionately, "Life is not lucid! There is no simplistic answer to being! Life is complicated and involved and has many faces, and who can say which face is reality?" But Life has only one Face, in truth, and that is the Face of God, and before Him there is no torturous path, no concealed passages, no multitude of answers, no confusion, no "This is the way, but on the other hand, this may be the way also." Man's mind, assisted by yours, becomes a hive of cells, each with a contradictory life entombed, each with an individual insistence, each with a different clamoring voice, each with a refuting reply. Only in the pure honey of truth is there one flow of sweetness, and there is naught so simple as honey.

Our Father does not dwell in the labyrinthine places. He lives in the sun where there is no concealment. But defiled in soul by you, man exclaims, "Where is God? I do not see Him! All is darkness. He has asked me, in this darkness, to be docile and accept as simply as does the beast of the field, or an infant in arms and at its mother's breast."

Yet the Lord has said so plainly, "You must be as children, to inherit the Kingdom of Heaven." Children do not question obliquely and in large words and in erudite phrases, nor do they accept the words of the old wise and reject the evidence that is before them. They see clearly and in whole, and not obscurely and in part.

You have told man that he has reason, and therefore he is like unto the gods and is aware of good and evil. But you have shown him only his own passions and his own desires and have urged him not to refuse them but to gratify them, for are they not his inherent nature? His reason is perverted by his intimate lusts, which you stimulate, and tempt in delectable form. He has no merit of his own, but only those merits granted by the Grace of God. Instinctively, in childhood, man recognizes this. It is only with learning that he glorifies that which he calls his "reason." So sad a little creature, so worthy of mercy, in his helplessness! The wisest of the men of Terra are the most stupid, the most refractory, the most blinded. But, are they the wise in truth? No, they are the most absolutely dumb and null. Only the simple are wise in the ways of wisdom, for when they ask they perceive the answer, and immediately. You have called this infantile, and men have listened to you through the ages. The spiral to them is fascinating and the more it curves about itself the more delighted they are, and they call it subtlety. The straight way is jejune to their contorted spirits. It lacks sophistication. Sad little man, strutting on his dung-heap and crowing defiantly at the sun as it rises, and often believing that without his crow the sun would not come up at all! At the worst, he is convinced that his dung-heap is the center of the universe and that the beat of his wings is heard to the farthest star.

Yet, Our Father chose to take on the flesh of this miserable small creature, this blind little mouse, this impudent manikin. This has angered and insulted you, as you have said so often through the eons. But God did not do this to torment you, as you say. He does not inflict suffering on His children. He had His reasons. You have written that if He does not erase the memory of man from all the planets, not only Terra, you will do it. That cannot be, unless He wills that you have your will. It is true that He sank ancient continents of Terra below the waters, and you exulted that the race was destroyed. But he rescued a few, and raised up other continents for their life and fertility and their ultimate hope. Your thunderbolts did not destroy the ark as it rose and fell on the vast and landless seas, nor were the inhabitants affrighted. It was not the will of Our Father that they be lost, but that they have life. There may come a day when God shall will that you have your way, but that day lives only in His mind, and you cannot know it.

You will have no pity. It was absurd of me to ask it, for I know your loathing for this bloody little ball of mud which committed the great crime of Deicide, and continues to commit it. Nevertheless, your very wrath against it gives me heart, for it was out of your love for Our Father that you have found Terra so outrageous. But even if God had chosen Madra, the most beautiful and splendid planet in all the universes, to be born of her, you would still have been fired with anger, for men live on Madra also, and mankind is your curse. You tempted man to fall ten thousand times ten thousand eons ago, and when he fell you fell with him also. He is your anathema as you are his. When he echoes you and blasphemes, it does not rejoice you. You would obliterate him for the very words you taught him! You would kill him for the evils he has embraced, though you invented those evils and filled his arms with them.

It is man's weakness before you that fills you with fury, yet you touch him with weakness in his mother's womb. When you say to him, "I am your only god, your only reality," and he bows before you in worship, you would smite him unto immediate death. Ah, Lucifer, once Star of Morning, you are the very father of man's incredible infamy, and while you demand his adoration you simultaneously demand that he die!

This is not a marvel to me, you who are a slave of slaves. But it is my sorrow. It is the sorrow of all your brothers also. But, who knows? One fair noon you may arise to the gates of Heaven on the ladder raised by men, and in striking on them you may cry, "Alleluia!"

Your brother, Michael

GREETINGS

to my brother, Michael, who is very tender and brave but, alas, most naïve:

Let me repeat as I have repeated always: If my entry into heaven must be accompanied by the souls of men, then I prefer my hells. At least there I torment my insulters and the insulters of Our Father, and this is an exuberant delight, one, I fear, you will never know.

Delight! Most assuredly! It is a joy which I cannot explain in words you would understand. Sufficient it is to say that I play with those souls as they played with their victims, and with the same mercilessness, only a thousand times enhanced. When they beseech me for pity I listen with ecstasy to their cries. Beasts, animals! To think that they, too, possess immortal life! They grovel before me and clutch my garments and I spurn them with my foot. Sometimes I admit a few of their wisest to my dark tabernacle and converse with them for the pleasure of listening to their stupidity, their arrant foolishness. Often I summon the great among them and urge them to speak of their fame on Terra, and it is an enormous amusement. They say to me, "I did not believe in you, nor in God, yet you manifestly are," and they marvel. I conjure their lives before them and I say, "There was I, in that apparition, when you planned this—or that—and you heard my voice and took rapture in it. Why did you harken to me, beast of beasts?" They answer, falling before my face, "I believed in nothing but myself and my own grandeur and my own will." But they believed in me.

They repent. But it is too late. They came to me, not through august sins which at least possess a measure of grandeur and imagination, but through sins so mean and contemptible that they are below the comprehension of the lowest of creatures on Terra. The serpent in the forest is not as poisonous as man, the rabid bat is not as mad and loathsome, the toothed shark is not so foul a scavenger. For none of these can lie. That is the prerogative of man only. Man always takes on the aspect of the serpent, the bat and the shark, and their habits. He is more dreadful than these, for he lacks their innocence and he knows what he does and he does it with enthusiasm and passion. It is through his lies that man comes to me, his lies of the flesh and the spirit, for untruth is a perversion and man is a pervert. He is the incarnation of the lie which is myself, and all the evil that he does is his corruption of truth.

You have asked for my pity on him. If I did not love you, Michael, I should feel myself forever insulted, and should then hate you.

My demons look upon the bountiful harvests of the souls of men who swarm through my fiery portals each hour, and they look with revulsion, for never, even among demons, was ever a spirit so malicious, so embued with hatred for his fellows, as the spirit of man. In his life on Terra he prates of love and esteems it with his tongue as the greatest of virtues. Yet never was a creature so loveless in his heart even when announcing love to the heavens. He crowds before the altars he has raised to God, and the lie nestles in his flesh, and the repudiation and disbelief, and even when he cries "Hosannah!" he chuckles in secret at his own perfidy. He loves that perfidy. He believes it gives him intellectual stature. He looks upon the crucified Lord and it needs no whisper from me to make him speak in his spirit and deny. He has many arguments, and they amuse him.

Not all men, you would say. Michael, Michael! That miserable little stream which flows to heaven is hardly a trickle compared with the great river that pours down to me!

You have not seen their appalled faces when they encounter me, who greet them thus: "Welcome to your spiritual home, you who have denied all things!" Still, it is very strange. Though they did not believe in Our Father, they truly believed in me, though they did not know it. You serve only that in which you believe, with knowledge or without knowledge. They would have been amazed to encounter you, Michael, and would have marveled. But they do not marvel at me. They recognize me at once. They have seen my face countless times, and they know all my lineaments. Nor is hell unfamiliar to them. They created a mirage of it on Terra, and they know every alley, every darksome passage, every icy lake, every mountain of fire, every gloomy shadow, every city of death, every pool of corruption. For while I established my hells, it was man who lifted up the walls and established the noisome places and lit the fires and froze the waters. It is, therefore, no mystery that he recognizes every path and sits down in his chosen spot to weep and repent. He built the house in which he dwells. At least, that is a species of freedom, for man did not build heaven. For in participation there is liberty, and complete liberty reigns in hell. Have I not said it through the ages! You have called my creatures slaves but slaves do not build to their design, and men build the designs of the infernos. It is by God's Grace when man reaches heaven, and not by his merits, and so perhaps not even his will. But men will to dwell with me, and where there is will there is freedom. Has not Our Father declared that, Himself? He is the Paradox of paradoxes.

There are no contradictions in hell. There are no wonders, for everything in hell is familiar to the souls of men. There is the complete security which men have always craved on Terra, but which Our Father lovingly denies them, for God is the Creator of infinite and opposing variety, delicious contrasts, innocent comicalities, awesome inequalities, enchanting absurdities, paradoxes, fearsome challenges, exciting uncertainties. This, I admit, stimulates color and splendor and merriment and marvelings and stern beauties and liveliness and trembling anticipations. But in hell there is nothing to anticipate; there is no variety, there is no insecurity. There are pain and boredom, and boredom is the most monstrous of punishments. Beside it, pain is a relief, so, despite the rumors of the ignorant on Terra, there is little pain in my hells except for futile regret. There is no future, yet there is time. Endless time, and endless sameness.

The pious in Terra speak only of the agonies of hell, and they exist for they are pleasure. Have they seen my glorious cities, bewitching, extravagant? They are filled with the delights of Terra, but immeasurably enhanced. Millions, newly arrived, look upon them with eagerness and smiles, and rush to inhabit them. The lavish city in which I live is a city that lived in the hot imaginations of men, filled with every satisfaction of their vile hearts, concupiscent lust of their flesh, every dream of their envious hearts. There are glittering houses heaped with gleaming treasures, and ballrooms and arenas and theaters and stadia, and shops to make any merchant weep with greed, and towering castles of every perversion and streets of magnitude filled with music, and tables everywhere crowded with saucy viands and bottomless vessels of wine, and demons to be slavish lackeys. There are vistas of heroic mountains like alabaster, and sparkling forests vibrating with song and valleys lush as velvet and rivers like gilt. Here souls of the damned are free to come and go, to sport, to converse, to play, to partake of all my captivations. They are free to argue their childish controversies, to engage in the pursuits that enthralled them on Terra, to discuss strange things with the inhabitants of worlds of which they never dreamed, to invent new theories and excited hypotheses, to "seduce" beautiful female demons. There is not an alluring vice that is denied them, not a passion which is not immediately gratified. Ah, I tell you, Michael, they often mistake hell for heaven at first!

But pleasure never changes in hell, never diminishes, can never aspire to greater diversions such as exalted meditation and reflection; never knows an end. Nothing is withheld; there is no struggle; there are no heart-burnings, no room for ambition and achievement. All is equal; all is accessible to every soul. There is no applause, for no soul exceeds another in stature. No face is different from any other face, nothing is unique or creative or deserving of acclaim. No soul is worthy, for all are worthless. Each is clad in the robes of doom—unchanging uniformity. Where one soul cannot excel another in any fashion ennui results and a mysterious terror, for God created all souls to strive and excel and thus be free and develop priceless individuality. But, it is my democracy.

At last, in despair and desperate boredom, my doomed pray for the less attractive portions of my sovereignty, where this is pain, and weeping and gnashing of teeth. Grief, at the final hour, becomes more desirable than pleasure, for it has needless ramifications. At the last I can engage these damned in my service—the seduction of souls yet living on Terra. At least there is some excitement in this! Envy and hatred and resentment are enlisted in my employ, for who of the damned can rejoice to see a soul escape him? What rejoicings there are in hell when more of the corrupted fall into the pit! If the Heavenly Hosts are joyous when a soul is saved, how much more are the damned joyous when a soul falls! Do not ask me why. Did I create man? His perverted mind often makes me recoil with disgust. You would say I perverted him. No, I only tempt.

With what glee my damned introduce the newly doomed to my hells! They look upon their dismayed faces and hug themselves with rapture. They peer for tears, and drink them avidly. They take the newly doomed by the hand and shout with happiness at the recoiling when horrors are confronted. This is the only satisfaction in hell, and it is a satisfaction most deeply encouraged.

Eventually, they all crave death and extinction. I am more compassionate than Our Father. I would often give them true death. But Our Father cursed them with eternal life, and so who is, in truth, the most merciless? God cannot withdraw from His own Law, therefore He cannot rescue my damned. When He gave immortality to man, did He know to what He had condemned him? Alas, alas, there are times when I would grant them death. Is your question then not answered? I am no Paradox, as is Our

Father. Had I created man—God forbid!—I should not have given him the free will to be damned if he desired. I should have made him obedient and docile, a gay little creature who could not know the difference between good and evil and therefore could have had no life but one brief day in the sun. I should have made him truly mortal, like a mayfly who takes pleasure in the noon and at sunset folds his wings and drifts into dust.

You once told me that hell is hell because no love can dwell there, and love is impossible. That is true. But love is passive and hatred is active, and man is always active like an insect which can never be still. Therefore, Michael, I shall win at last, for man is invariably enthusiastic and zealous, and languishes only when there is nothing to hate.

Your brother, Lucifer

GREETINGS

to my brother, Lucifer, who weeps at his triumphs:

Always you have fulminated because one thing was denied you in Heaven: the Knowledge of what lay in Our Father's Mind. None knows His Mind, not I, not Gabriel. We do not resent that; that was reserved for you. We dared not question His Knowledge, lest it blind us. But you were impatient and inquisitive and you bestowed these miseries upon man.

You have written that you are more merciful than Our Father, for you would have denied man immortal life. You would also have denied him Heaven. You would have denied him the one thing which makes him higher than the other animals on all the other worlds besides Terra: free will. Better it is for a man even to be damned than to be without that awesome gift! At least he had his choice. That alone gives him dignity, whether in Heaven or in hell, and in spite of all your efforts, my poor brother, you cannot deprive the damned of dignity. They share your immortal existence, and for that you cannot forgive them. They have their garment of eternal life.

Even a damned soul who grieves for what he lost is more than a body which expires with the breath. Would you prefer not to be, Lucifer?

I look upon the constant striving in Heaven with pleasure and affection. There is a perpetual coming and going of angels and the souls of the saved with news of new planets and universes and the wonders upon them. There is endless laughter and excitement and exchange of opinion and conjecture. Was it not the Christ who said that human ear has not heard and human eye has not seen the marvels which God has prepared for those who love Him?

Do I need to recall to you the aspect of Heaven? Eternal noon, but not an unchanging noon. No vista remains the same. No vision of the eye is static. The only constant is love between angel and man and God and angel and God and man. All else changes, and always there is anticipation and work. Work is not an affliction, as human hearts believe it is. When God "condemned" man to work He bestowed the next holiest gift after free will. Labor is prayer and achievement, and the uncertainty of the achievement. Beauty is always in the process of becoming, but is never fully attained. Joy is in the next turning, but the next turning promises greater joy. Love is never completely satisfied in Heaven, except for the surety of the Love of God. It strains forever, and happily, after greater fulfillments.

If a soul is weary after its sojourn on any of the worlds, it may rest in green shadows and peace until its weariness is spent. Then it must engage in the work of God, which is never completed. It so engages with eagerness and with a pleasure that is never satisfied. Does a soul desire to create marvelous sunsets or dawns on any world? It is given into its hands, for the greater glory of God. The soul paints the skies with the calm and stately morning or the pensive quietude of evening. It colors the flowers of the field and gives the grain its gold. If it is concerned with wonders that baffled it in life, then it pursues the answer to the wonders and it becomes luminous with satisfaction when the answer is finally perceived. But still other wonders beckon it on, and tantalize it.

Was a soul without the love of men on the worlds and did it languish for that love? It is poured into its immortal hands in Heaven and is appeased. Did it hope on the earths that it would see the faces of the lost beloved? It so sees and knows that never again can there be parting or ennui with love, itself. Did it long for children to embrace, when children were denied? Its arms are rich with children in Heaven. Was it homeless before its ascent? It can create for itself the home of its lost dreams, whether humble or a palace. Did it desire to serve God to the utmost while in flesh, yet could not fulfill that desire? The fulfillment is its own, ranging the endless universes and inspiring the sorrowful and lifting up the hearts of the sad and soothing the pain of the innocent, and bringing good news to those who dwell in darkness. It can whisper in the winds and bring knowledge in the twilights and hope in the dawns. Each soul that it helps save and bring safely to God is an occasion for triumph, and its fellows triumph with it.

All of which a man innocently dreamed in flesh is his at home, whether simple or magnificent. Best of all he grows in accomplishment. Always, there is the divine discontent, and never the security of hell. Always, angels and men must strive in Heaven. There is not one congregation, for in congregations there is conformity and the soul cannot exist in sameness. Each soul is an individual, and resembles no other, and serves no other. It serves its own need, and God is its need, and though it attains God it never fully envelops or knows Him. There is its most splendid dissatisfaction, its happiness. For what is completely possessed is a weariness. Victory is nothing when victory is entirely attained. You have seen the misery of conquerors on all the worlds, when there was nothing else to conquer. But none conquers in Heaven save God, and who knows if He fully conquers?

Above all, in Heaven, there is no exhaustion, no tiredness of spirit, no repletion. There is eternal youth, and endless speculation. You have said that love is passive. If it is, then it is not love at all, but only selfish desire or a momentary engrossment. It is peaceful, and that is true, but it is not the peace of death. It is surety, but still it is not the surety of the grave. It must eternally be sought and eternally found, with new aspects and new delights. The music of Heaven is the voices of those who have seen a new face in love and marvel that they had not seen it before.

The City of God is not like unto your city, O Lucifer, for there is no gross pleasure in it, no obscene appetites.

All that was beautiful and beguiling and enchanting on the worlds is greatly magnified in Heaven, and always changing, offering new enticements. It is never the same, while it is always the same. You will scornfully say again that that is a paradox, but there is infinite delight in paradoxes. Only Absolutes are rigid, and rigidity is the true death of the spirit. But one Absolute reigns in Heaven and the planets, and that is the Absolute of God's love. All else moves with the soul and is part of it. One veil is lifted but to reveal another veil of an even more enthralling color. Pursuit of the unattainable is the climate of Heaven.

There is no end of knowledge in Heaven, no end of learning. The soul pursues new knowledge and learns forever. It does not stand like a marble image confronting changelessness. Its face is eternally lit with the fires and the colors of new universes and new aspirations and new adventures. It clamors to *know*. Yet, it can never know completely, and that is its reward. God is like an earthly father who constantly places new riddles before his children, and smiles as they eagerly guess its secrets and learn its answers. There are always new books to read, new wonders to excite the imagination, new vistas to explore.

When you were in Heaven you declared that this finally wearied you, for, you said, Heaven was like a ball of silk which was never fully unwound and there was no hope of the unwinding. In short, you wished to make Heaven a hell, where there is absolute fulfillment, and there is nothing more to be attained. A state of stasis is surely hell, as you have discovered to your sorrow. You wished to sleep, you said, and you rested on your great white wings of light, but you did not sleep. You wished to peer and understand that which is not understandable, even by archangels. You desired the ultimate. Alas, Lucifer, you have attained it. Your city resounds with success. Why, then, are you not content?

Today new worlds in time were born about one of my largest stars in my Galaxy. You will, without doubt, visit them and attempt to corrupt their people. I pray that you will fail, not only for the sake of God but for your own sake.

Your brother, Michael

GREETINGS

to my brother, Michael, who believes that in much repetition there are new revelations:

Your last letter to me seems addressed more to your new worlds, with which God has endowed you, rather than to me who knows Heaven as well as you, and perhaps much more, for was I not created before you? True, there are no Absolutes in Heaven save for Our Father, Who is all Absolutes. Therein I find a tediousness, and, paradox of paradoxes! There is a strange similarity between Heaven and hell: Change that is not really change, though you would disagree. Each morning my damned say, "This is another day!" But they discover that it is the same as the day before. In Heaven, there is no time. Surely, that is a greater weariness. My damned do not attain, for there is nothing to attain. Your holy souls do not attain, for total attainment is not possible. The soul strains, whether in Heaven or hell. If there is a singular difference I have yet to discern it. You would speak of the joy in the Beatific Vision, and do I not know it? I saw it first, my dear brother! But if even archangels are not to know its supreme secrets, wherein lies the satisfaction? To know that one can never know all appears to me, at times, to be hell, itself. At least my damned know all there is to know of hell, and my nature. There are no hidden corners, and if there are no fresh delights there are no fresh mysteries and no terrors, however sublime. This condition has always seemed the most desirable among men—and have I not given it to them?

There is an answer for every question in hell. My demons are solicitous. No soul asks without a reply. If the reply is mundane and possesses no novelty—did not man wish that for himself during the time of his mortal life? Nothing affrights these miserable wretches more than a hint that a strangeness is about to appear, yet they bewail —after a space—the sameness of hell. On all their worlds they struggle for the very condition they find in my hells —no disturbing variety, no uncertainty, no danger, no test of courage, no challenge, and no enigmas. They considered this the most marvelous of existences. Once assured of it in hell, however, they are agonized. I have always said that human souls were pusillanimous and blind, and contradictory.

Certainly, in hell, there is no free will, for the damned relinquished it on their worlds. This torment has been denied them by me. Therefore, they cannot will to climb to Heaven by self-denial, by contemplation, by worship, by dedication, by acts of faith and charity. These attributes shriveled in them during their lives, or were rejected scornfully by them in moods of risible sophistications. They can desire to possess them now, but I would keep them safe and warm, as Our Father never kept them so! So, they can will nothing. They can only accept the pleasures—and the pains—I bestow on them.

In Heaven, however, free will is fully released. The ability to reject, to deny, remains with archangels, angels and the souls of the saved. The gift of repudiation is still with them and the possibility of disobedience. Is that not most frightful? What insecurity! What danger! My damned remain with me in eternal slavery because in life they desired only safety, and lacked the fire of adventure, though, God knows, they protested enough on their worlds! But what did they protest? Inequality, which is the variety of God. Instability, which is the light of the universes. Uneasiness of mind, which is the soul of philosophy. Apparent injustices, which are the goad of the spirit. Vulnerability to life and other men, which is a charge to become invulnerable through Faith in God. The presence of suffering or misfortune—but these are a call for the soul to put on armor and serenity. They demanded of their rulers that they remain in constant co-

coons, silky and guarded by earthly authority. They did not ask for wings to soar into the sunlight, and the ominous threats of full existence. They rejected freedom for hell. Certainly, they cried for freedom on their worlds, but it was freedom only to live happily without the freedom to be divinely unhappy.

I have satisfied all these lusts of men. Strange, is it not, that my hells, though the ultimate success of the dreams of men, are filled with weeping? And strange, is it not, that they still do not believe in the existence of God? But then, they never did; they believed only in me. They cannot will to believe in God. They see absolute reality about them now, which was their will in life. I will not pretend that I do not understand them, for was it not I who promised them all without work and without striving?

But lately I asked of a newly descended soul which had much acclaim on Terra: "What was your greatest desire on your world, you who were applauded by rulers and admired by your fellowmen?"

He replied, "Justice for all," and put on a very righteous expression.

That was admirable, for who does not admire justice, even I? But I probed him. He declared that in his earthly view all men deserved what all other men possessed, whether worthy or not. "They are men, so they are equal, and being born they have a right to the fruits of the world, no matter the condition of their birth or the content of their minds, or their capacities." I conducted him through the pleasures of my hell, and he was delighted that no soul was lesser in riches than another, and that every soul had access to my banquets and my palaces, no soul was distinguishable from another, none possessed what another did not possess. Every desire was immediately gratified, he discovered. He smiled about him joyfully. He said, "Here, justice is attained!"

Then he saw that no face was joyful, however mean or lofty its features. He remarked, wonderingly, on the listlessness of my damned, and how they strolled emptily through thoroughfares filled with music and through streets wherein there was not a single humble habitation.

He heard the cries of pleasure over my laden tables, and then heard them silenced, for there was no need now for food and where there is no need there is no desire and no enjoyment. He saw that the poorest on earth were clothed in magnificence and jewels, yet they wept the loudest. He was no fool. He said, "Satiety." True, I answered him, but satiety can live only in the presence of total equality. He pondered on this while I led him to the seat of thousands of philosophers, and he sat down among them. But, as there is no challenge in hell, and no mystery, there can be no philosophy. That night he came to me on his knees and begged for death. I struck him with my foot, and said, "O man, this was the hell you made, and this was the desire of your heart, so eat, drink, and be merry."

He attempted to hang himself, in the manner of Judas, and I laughed at his futility. I meditated that above all futility is the climate of hell.

He said to me, in tears, "Then, if you are, then God exists."

"That does not follow," I replied to him. "But, did you not deny Him on Terra? Did you not speak of supraman, and man-becoming, and the ultimate glorification of man on earth, without God?"

"I did not see God among men," he said, wringing his hands.

"You did not look," I said. "You were too dull in your human arrogance and too enamored of humanity. You never denounced your fellows for their lusts and their cruelties. You told them they were only 'victims.' You refused to look upon their nature, for you denied the infinite variety and capacities of nature. To you, one man was as good as any other man, and equally endowed, for the foolish reason that he had been born. You saw no saints, and no sinners. It was only a matter of environment, though the proof was all about you that environment is a mere shading or tint on the soul, and is not destiny. You denied that men have gifts of the spirit, often above those of other men. In truth, you denigrated those gifts of striving and wonder. You denied free will. Everything evil that happened to a man was only the result of his fellowmen's lack of justice. You denied the reality of good and evil, the ability to make a choice. In short, you denied life, itself."

"Then God in truth does exist?" he asked, after a moment's miserable thought.

"That you will never know," I said. "But rejoice! All your dreams are fulfilled here. Delight yourself. Behold, there are beautiful female demons here, and banquets and sports and pleasures and soft beds and lovely scenes and all whom you had wished, in life, you had known. Converse with them."

"There is no desire in me," he said. "I want nothing."

"You are surely in hell," I replied, and I left him weeping.

God pursues them even in hell. Or, does He, my beloved Michael? Grief is the gift of God. But He will not have my damned! For they have no will to rise to Him. Or, do they? This thought arouses my anger. I have my domain uniquely mine. I will not permit Him here, though once He came. I must discuss that with you another time.

But let us speak of your new worlds, which you mentioned in your last letter.

Pandara, among the dozen about the enormous and fiery blue sun, interests me. Our Father struck six women and six men from the jeweled dust, and gave them the Sacrament of marriage. I must congratulate God, for these creatures are fairer than many others. Their flesh resembles rosy alabaster, and their hair is bright and sparkling, and their eyes are green and full of light. They will have eternal youth if they do not fall. They frolic and work in the warm and turquoise radiance, where there are no seasons because Pandara moves upright in her long slow orbit about her parent sun. There will be no fierceness of storm or calamities of nature—unless these creatures fall. There will be joyous labor and eager participation in life, and life without end in the forests full of red and purple and golden flowers, and about the lucent rivers and the mother-of-pearl lakes. There will be cities of song and learning. There will be adventure and delight.

I have seen the red peaks of mountains, and the dawns like benedictions and the sunsets like Heaven, itself. There is no disease here, no hunger, no sorrow, no pain, no death. There is knowledge of God, and God moves among them, and they feel His presence and His love.

Alas, God has also endowed them with free will.

That is my opportunity.

The women and the men are as young as life. I can bring them age and evil and disease and death and violence and hatred and lusts. Six women, and six men. What shall I do?

Shall I introduce a seventh man, my Damon, who seduced so many on other worlds, and on miserable Terra, where he seduced Eve and Helen of Troy and millions of other women? He is a beautiful angel, full of gaiety and subtlety and delectabilities. His conversations are absorbing and delicious. His inventions of the flesh are luscious and charming; his concupiscences are sweeter than any fruit. Few women have ever rejected him. His very touch, his smile, is beguiling, and he is all that is male. How can any woman resist him?

If introduced on Pandara the women will reflect that he is far more beautiful than their husbands, and that he does not toil in the fields and that his discourses are wondrous and mysterious, and that he hints of joys they have never experienced before. Sad, is it not, that even Our Father stands at bay before a woman? Who can know the intricacies of a female heart, and its secret imaginings? Damon knows these intricacies, and winds them about his fingers like silver or darksome threads. He can persuade almost any woman into adultery.

It needs but Damon to destroy Pandara.

Or, perhaps, I will send Lilith, my favorite female demon, to the men of Pandara, that beautiful planet. She seduced Adam and Pericles and Alexander and Julius Caesar and so many rulers on Terra now. Who is so lovely as Lilith? Once she graced the Courts of Heaven and all looked on her beauty with awe. She has a thousand astounding forms, and each one more gorgeous than another. She is never oppressive, never demanding. She is

yielding and soft and attentive. She follows; she never
leads. When she speaks her voice is like celestial music.
Each attitude resembles a statue of sublime glory. She
says to men, "How wondrous you are, how unique, how
intellectual, how far above me in understanding!" She is
femininity itself, easily conquered, easily overcome by
flattery, easily induced to surrender. She has only to beckon and men rush to her with cries of lust and desire.

Damon or Lilith?

Strange to remark, men are less susceptible to determined seduction than women. Damon can offer women
mysteries and endless amusement, and what woman can
spurn mystery or amusement? They love the secret dark
places, the moon, the whispered hotness, the promise of
uniqueness and adoration. Women do not crave power;
they are not objective. Truth to them is relative. Is this
evil or good? Women in their minds can create a confusion, and this, on so many worlds, they have bequeathed
to their sons. A woman can resolve all things in her mind
and make so many splendid compromises. If the women
of Pandara look upon Damon there will be rivalries for
his smiles and attention, the lonely male they will yearn
to take to their breasts when their husbands are absent.
There is a certain doggedness in husbands which women
find full of ennui.

On the other hand, there is Lilith, who is always am-
biguous and never captured. Men seek after the uncap-
tured, the unattainable, which, alas, is the climate of
Heaven. Lilith is always pursued but never caught. What
man can resist Lilith, who never argues, never complains,
is always complaisant and always fresh and dainty? Her
conversation never demands that a man ponder, or question. Men, I have discovered, detest women who pose
challenges of the mind and the soul. They are engrossed
in the flesh to the deepest extent, therefore they are simple, however their pretensions to intellect. They dislike
women who ask "Why?" They turn from women with serious faces and furrowed brows. They wish only to play,
to gratify themselves in moments of leisure. They find
their wives always at hand, and women's conversation is

usually concerned with children and the dull affairs of daily living. The women say, "How are the crops, or the cattle? How is our present treasure?"

But Lilith says, "Let us frolic and rejoice in the sun and weave garlands of roses and drink wine and laugh and discover comedies. Above all, let us embrace each other." This is the exact opposite of the conversation of wives, and so is irresistible.

Too, women are sedulous in the seeking of God, which is the other side of their nature. Men can endure just so much of God, and just so much discussion of Him. After that, they seek love and physical activity or their little philosophies. Or sleep. Men love slumber, though women resist it. Man reasons, woman conjectures. Therefore, man wearies first. He is always yawning in the very midst of feminine discourse.

Considering this, I believe Damon will be the most potent in Pandara, as he was in the majority of worlds. Women do not fall lightly. Eve gave much thought before she ate of the Forbidden Tree. (Adam was merely vaguely aware of it, and, as it was forbidden, he usually ignored it. Men are slaves to law.) Damon adores the struggle in the female spirit, for while seductible it thinks of God. Lilith often complains that men are so easily the victims of their flesh, so there is no serious enticement, no arduous pursuit. In concupiscence, men never think of God at all.

I shall send Damon, the beautiful, the most alluring of male demons.

(If I seem contradictory concerning the nature of humanity, sweet Michael, it does not follow that I am inconsistent. I have written that men are less susceptible than women to seduction, but that is on the score of sensibility. A woman cannot be seduced by raw sensuality; her mind and spirit must be engaged also, and she must be convinced that in some fashion the purity of love is involved. She must feel the wings of her soul expand, so that all is well lost for love, itself. It takes on itself, in her mind, the aspect of the eternal, the immutable. So, women are an excitement to Damon. But the purely female, like Lilith, cannot be resisted by men, who see nothing eternal in marital love, nothing sanctified, however the words they repeated by rote. A woman is just an encounter to a man. She can be successfully resisted only if she is intelligent and only if she asks questions, and only if she demands that the situation be permanent. Woman must be seduced through her most delicate emotions. Man alone can be seduced if no spiritual emotions are present at all. Damon was forced to converse with Eve to the point of exhaustion before she ate of the fruit which was forbidden. Had Lilith approached Adam, the deliciousness of the fruit would have needed only to be described. I made an error there—or was it the will of God? How He eternally intrudes!)

Yes, my choice will be Damon. He will be elegant to the women of Pandara. He will not openly seduce. He will treat them as equals, yet not so equal that it diminishes his masculine power. He will declare that their souls and their minds entrance him, that above all women they are the most ravishing. He will talk poetry with them hour after hour; he will never be bored, as husbands are bored. He will indicate the beauties on their world, and will strike attitudes, but not effeminate ones. He will tenderly entwine flowers in their bright hair. He will kiss their hands, and show his muscles at the same time. If they leap with enjoyment, he will leap higher. He will pursue, and offer them ardent embraces. He will discuss their natural problems with them, with manly indulgence. If they become pettish, in the way of women, he will seize them in his strong arms and quiet their mouths with his own. At the last, as if tired of play, he will lift them up and run with them to some silent glade and forcibly take them, ignoring their hypocritical cries and their beating hands. Above all, he will pretend that they, themselves, seduced him with their beauty and reduced him to distraction. What woman can believe that she is without allurement, either of the body or the mind?

I am sad for you, Michael, my brother. Pandara is already lost. I am sending Damon tonight to the women of your beautiful planet. I will reserve Lilith for later, when the race is fallen. She will convince men that lust is more delightful than reason, and feminine charms more to be desired than sanctity, or duty. The flesh, she will say, has its imperative, but where is the imperative of the soul—if it exists at all? The flesh is tangible and lovely. Who would forego it for the transports of the spirit? The man who would do that, she will inform her victims, is no man at all and is not potent.

In short, he is a eunuch. What man does not believe that with a perceptive woman he will be forever virile, despite age or change? Lilith will introduce man to perversions and to atrocities. She will guide him into cruelties which women can never imagine. She will cloud his mind. She will darken his soul against God, while he basks in her arms.

I anticipate Pandara and her sister worlds, for they are now inhabited with a new race, fairer and more intelligent than Terra, among others. Terra, in particular, has always had a certain and sickening mediocrity of intellectual climate, now stimulated by those who designate themselves as "intellectuals." Terra dutifully conforms to what her race calls non-conformity. Rare has been the man in her history who was truly individual, and those men were either murdered for their purity of soul or, in despair at the race, became its glorious assassins. In general, the history of Terra has been stupid if frightful, predictable if dreadful. The souls of Terra which descend to me give even hell disagreeable moments, for they are ciphers. Yet, on the other hand, they form a special torment to those souls from other worlds who are more intellectually endowed, and it is very amusing. The men from other worlds have even, in hell, attempted to lift up the intelligence of the men of Terra, to no avail, but to much comedy for my demons. There have been desperate but fruitless classes in the sciences and the arts for the men of Terra, and they have always failed, and there have been cries, "These souls are not truly human! They are impermeable!" True, but I always discourage such outcries with the formula of "democracy." This ritualistic word silences the souls of other worlds, if it tortures them, for was it not their own invention?

My dear brother. In the golden twilight of Pandara I visited your magnificent planet. There I discovered you in a great purple garden, conversing with Our Father, and your voice was full of laughter and gaiety and innocent abandon, for you were rejoicing in the beauty of where you found yourself and were exchanging jests with Him. (The gaiety of Heaven! I found it disturbing at times, for is existence not always serious and earnest and Engaged with Larger Matters?) I did not see Our Father, but He saw me. I felt His majestic presence, and I covered my face with my wings. But still, I knew His penetrating eyes and how can I bear them, so full of reproach and sorrow? It is not my fault. He does not understand, and, alas, it is possible that He never will. He did not speak to me, but He spoke to you, and I heard your voices and your mirth. The green dolphins of the seas appeared to be amusing you.

I have had another thought: When Pandara has fallen I will send one of my favorite demons to her, whose name is Triviality. You know him well. You have seen him in his activity on thousands of planets, and he is more deadly than Damon and Lilith combined. I will write of him another time.

But first Damon and Lilith will have your Pandara and her sister planets. I must not be censored. Men do these things to themselves, and not I. I entice. I indulge men's deepest desires. But I can move only in an atmosphere of free will, which God created. Will He save Pandara also?

Your brother, Lucifer

GREETINGS

to my brother, Lucifer, who, as the great archangel he is, gives courteous warnings of his dire intentions:

We are excessively pleased that you have informed us that you will send Damon to Pandara, to seduce her six women. (Ah, I remember Damon well! An angel of mischief and wit and jests. Alas, Heaven is the poorer for the absence of that gay spirit.)

So, we have taken precautions against Damon and Lilith. Unfortunately, we had to introduce suspicion into that vast paradise. We should have preferred that entire innocence prevail, but one remembers that Our Father set, in the midst of Eden, a Forbidden Tree. Suspicion, entering into Pandara, will awaken the power of free will, and a healthy mistrust.

Therefore, I appeared to the wives of Pandara, the innocent treasures!—and informed them that they were with child, which pleased them mightily. However, I mourned, they and their unborn children were in deadly danger. A beautiful female demon, one Lilith, who destroyed the souls of millions upon millions of other men, would soon enter the azure light of their planet to seduce their husbands and lead their husbands into unspeakable pleasures and lust, thus insuring that for a time, at least, those husbands would forget their wives and abandon their little nestlings. The husbands would romp with Lilith, neglectful of the duties of hearth, home and bed and field, and they would love her with madness and be so smitten of her charms that they would regard their wives with distaste and possibly revulsion. Worse still, the harvests would be neglected, the cattle unfed, the roofs unsealed, and whereof would wives and children then eat and how would they sleep, unprotected from the rains and the winds?

A woman may forgive her husband a romp in the shadowy forests, but she will not forgive him the sufferings of her children, nor will she forgive the great insult to her own beauty and desirability. The ladies said to me, "Is this Lilith fairer than I?" And I replied, "Assuredly, she is the fairest of women, for all she is a demon, and are not maddening women demons? Though you are lovely to behold, my little ones, Lilith in contrast will cast a dust of ugliness upon you in your husbands' eyes. But above all, she will shatter the peace and joy of your planet, and bring age upon your faces, and wrinkles, and dim the green fire of your eyes, and she will bring death upon your children and disease and storms and darkness and furies."

"What, then, shall we do, to preserve our planet, our homes, our youth, and our life and our children?" the ladies implored me.

"Ah," I told them, "men are susceptible to ladies of no virtue and no matronly attributes! They are like adorable children, wanton at heart but in need of protection, and the careful supervision of alerted wives. They will stretch forth their hands for the flying hair of a woman of no sturdy consequence, and they will dance with her in the moonlight and garland her head with flowers and press their cheeks against her breast, and drink of wine deeply with her. She will laugh and sing and play, and a wise matron understands how these things can lure men from their duties. She will becloud the minds of your husbands so that they will think of pleasure and not the granaries, laughter in the sun and not of weak roofs, roses in the glades and not of wool to be sheared. There is a certain weakness in men that inclines them to frivolity and dallying, and Lilith will exploit that weakness and entice your husbands from your sides. She will, if you slacken your watchfulness for a moment and do not regard your husbands with some severity."

"We will be watchful, O, Lord Michael!" the wives

promised me, and there was an ominous green fire in
their eyes which I momentarily regretted, thinking of
their husbands. If Life will be slightly less pleasant and
agreeable hereafter for the men of Pandara, and a little
more restricted and scentless, and if their ways are
watched by their wives and their restlessness suppressed
at once—and if their gambols and songs are more scruti-
nized than before—is this not better than death and sin
and age and disease and sorrow, not to mention the harsh
tongues of betrayed wives? I have observed that men can
endure great hardships and adversities with considerable
calm, but they cannot endure for long the smite of a
woman's less affectionate remarks, and her acid conversation at midnight when they would prefer to sleep. You
have been merciful in your hells at least, Lucifer, for
women are not encouraged to be astringent there nor
righteously abusive.

I then repaired to the husbands of Pandara, and when
they had risen from their knees at my consent, I said to
them, "Glorious is your planet, beloved sons of God, my
dear brothers, and fair are her skies and rich are her
fields and splendid will be your cities. Handsome are your
faces and strong are the rosy muscles of your arms, and
your wives rejoice in you."

"It is so, Lord!" they cried in jubilation, and I smiled
at the happiness in their eyes and loved them dearly for
the male spirit is a little less complicated than the female
and somewhat more naïve. It has an innocence, even in
paradise, beyond the innocence of women who, even in
paradise, are given to reflection, and are less trusting.

"But alas," I said to the boys, "your joy is threatened,
for you have free will, as you know, and alas again, so do
your wives. They have it even more, and that is one of
the mysteries of the Almighty, before Whom we shade
our faces in awe. Men are often slave to habit, virtuous
or unvirtuous, but women have few habits at all and so
are easily led astray into novelties. Your wives, though
with child, will not always be with child. They will have
moments of leisure. While leisure for a man is a quiet
resting or an innocent pastime or a running after balls or

a climbing of trees for the fruit, or just sleeping, leisure for a woman is the veriest temptation. She has a seeking mind, and what she seeks out is not always immaculate. Too, she is usually enamored of herself, and searches for compliments. Have you not already discovered this for yourselves?"

They considered, then wrinkled their pure brows. "It is true," one of them said, and I was sorry that I had recalled his wife to him, but it was necessary, as you will doubtless agree. "My wife often sits by a limpid pool and admires her countenance, and then looks far off and dreams. I wonder of what she is dreaming."

"Your wives will all have dreams very soon," I told them, "and none of them will be virtuous. None of them will be concerned for the husband who labors in the fields and the forests and who tends cattle and returns dutifully home to his children and sits soberly on his hearth. On the contrary! They will be dreams which I hesitate to speak of, for women's minds are somewhat less decorous and guileless than men's, even on Pandara. The indelicacy of a woman's thoughts would bring a flame to the cheek of even the burliest man. You have observed that nature is not always delicate?"

"It is true," said the lads, with a worry in their eyes which saddened me.

"And women are far closer to nature than are you, for all you labor in the fields and the forests. There is a certain earthiness in women which is sometimes an embarrassment to husbands, a certain lustiness of the flesh that is not always easily satisfied. If I am incorrect, I beg your forgiveness."

"You are correct, Lord," said the simple ones.

"Then, indeed alas," I said. "For unto your wives there will be sent from the very depths of hell an evil but most beautiful male demon, one Damon. I know him well! He has seduced endless millions of women on other planets, as fair and as matronly as your own, and as busy—with dreams. He is full of novelties and enticements, and adores women and finds them overwhelmingly fascinating —which you not always do. Their conversation never wearies him; he is attentive and glorious. As he never labors, except to do mischief, he is not weary at sundown, as you are weary. As he is a demon and not a man, he does not sleep, and women are notable for being active at night. And dreaming. He converses. You have no idea what a menace to husbands is a conversing man! But women find it distracting.

"You love your wives. Soon, they will bear children. However, when Damon comes to seduce them with fair words, with exciting discourse, with flatteries and ardencies, and will shine the beauty of his countenance upon them and jest with them until they are weak with laughter and adoration, they will forget you and your children, and will race with him to flowery dells and into dim lush spots—and will then betray you for his kisses and his lusts. Then will your children cry for a maternal breast, and then will there be no dishes upon the table to appease your hungers, and no arms to sustain you in your beds. You will be veritable orphans, abandoned and alone, left to weep among the wreckages of your households, and the uncleaned pots and the stale bread. Is that not a fate to weep about, and to pray never afflicts you?"

"Oh, Lord!" they cried in despair, "that is a fate worse than death!"

I had to confess, "Not entirely. Let us not be extravagant. Incidentally, Damon has a voice that is irresistible, and what woman can resist a musical voice if it is also masculine? Damon is all masculinity; he is never weary. His muscles never ache. His foot never lags. He never frowns, if dinner is a little late. He is also never hungry, as you are hungry, and you know how impatient wives are with the honest hunger of a man. They remark that men's bellies seem bottomless. Correct me if I am wrong."

"You are correct, Lord," they said, with dismalness and alarm.

"As Damon does not seek a woman with forthrightness, and with sleep in mind thereafter—as you do—he will dally with a woman after love, until she is ready and eager for his embraces again. Whereas you, my dear little ones, wish to turn on your pillows in preparation for the next day's work. Damon never asks, "Do you love me?" as your wives ask, until you yawn for very boredom. He constantly assures the creature of his immediate affection that never has he loved a woman so before, and how rapturous are her kisses and perfumed her flesh. Do you say all this to your wives?"

"No, Lord," they said dolorously.

"You might practice it sometime," I told them with affection. "It will be somewhat hard to keep it in mind, but it is worth practice. After all, a lady must have her assurances also, and if her husband considers, or pretends to consider, her a flower among women, a gem above gems, she will lure him with daintier dishes and a more compliant behavior, even when he is abrupt. She will forgive him certain rudenesses of manner, for is he not the most magnificent of—well, poets? She will forebear to scold him for forgetfulnesses. She will seek his gratifications and comforts above all over matters, even children. His little weaknesses, in themselves, will make her believe they are lovable, and in the nature of men—which they are, of course. Have you been derelict, my brothers?" I asked, detecting a flicker of sheepishness on their faces.

"We have not always been patient with the vagaries of women," one confessed.

"Be patient. For one comes who will have all the patience in the world and will never weary. Not only will he seduce your wives, so that all the horrors I have described will come upon you, but he will bring old age and death to you, and flagging of strength, and disease and pain. Worse, he will sharpen your women's tongues, and nothing is more deadly."

"How can we escape such a dreadful fate?" they cried.

"I hesitate," I said, "being a male spirit of considerable compassion, to cast doubts into your minds. But let that man beware who has never doubted a woman, even his wife! Men are trustful, when it involves women, and that is a momentous mystery which I will not even attempt to explore. I do not advise distrust as a general climate of the mind. That can inspire eventual cynicism and lovelessness. But a reasonable distrust is prudent. And one knows the weaknesses of women. Do we not?"

"Certainly!" they exclaimed, positive that they had always known female weaknesses, though the fact had only just occurred to them, alas.

"Then, be watchful for Damon. Never leave your wives long unguarded, especially in the soft eventides and when the moons are shining. Do not dally in the fields and the forests and the hills and the meadows as the sun begins to go down. Do not let anything draw you aside, even if it appears exciting and wondrous and new—and, probably beautiful, itself. For, if you delay, Damon will appear on your thresholds at home, and you may return to an empty household. A moment's delight can cost you a whole life's industry and hope and peace. And, again, it will bring you death and suffering."

Of course, one of the younger lads became curious. "Of what nature is this wonder and delight you speak of, Lord, which could delay our return to our households?"

"Ah," I said, "it is but another shadow of evil. Let us not discuss it. You are men; you are strong. And you have your honor to guard—in the shape of your wives."

It is not sensible, as you know, Lucifer, to describe a handsome man to a woman or a lovely woman to a man, human nature being what it is, even on the Eden which is Pandara.

"We will guard our honor and the honor of our households and the safety of our children and the purity of our wives!" shouted the innocent ones, raising their fists high in a solemn oath. "Ever shall we be watchful of our women, understanding their weaknesses and their frail natures and their susceptibilities to temptation!"

I gave them my blessing and departed. They have been warned. Suspicion has been introduced into the turquoise daylight and the silver and lilac nights. But was not fear of the Forbidden Tree introduced on Terra? Even in Heaven the dread of transgressing the Law is with us—for we have free will. There are times, I am afraid, Lucifer, that I sympathize with your plaint that men were also given free will, but as they are of the essence of the Father they could not, in consistency, have been denied. In Heaven we are unequally perfect, in accordance with the ability to be perfect inherent in our natures. And that brings me to another subject you discussed in your last letter: Equality, which pervades hell.

In Heaven, there is Equity, which is an entirely different matter.

The laws of men are harsh and inflexible, especially those on the fallen planets. The same crime brings the same punishment, allegedly to all men, though I have noticed that it depends on the influence or the treasure the accused man possesses in entirely too many instances, or whether his appearance is or is not pleasing to a jury of his peers—a word that strikes ill on my ear because no man has peers. But I digress. The same situation prevails in hell—equality of treatment no matter the soul. However, in Heaven, as I have mentioned, there is Equity, based on the Natural Law that some men are superior to others, and some angels less than others, in virtue, in devotion, in piety, in dedication, love and courage and goodness. Equity does not abolish law; it intelligently deals with it, and its inflexibility.

Therefore, spirits in Heaven, angel or man, are rewarded in direct ratio to their accomplishments, which are governed by their will. Man, as we know, cannot earn merit during his lifetime on the grosser material of the planets, unless he has not fallen. But fallen men are incapable of earning merit, for their sin has thrown a wall of human impotence between them and their Creator. Only the Grace of Our Father can give merit to fallen men, and that merit is given by the men's own acts, through their faith and their desire to receive Grace, through their repentance and their penance, through their acceptance of Grace, itself. You know this; it is a matter which has enraged you through time, so I beg your forgiveness for boring you.

The saved among men, who desired to be saved and therefore had placed themselves in a position to receive Grace, differ enormously in the degree of their natures and their virtues, as well as in their wills and their sins. A murderer in hell, and a wanton thief, are treated equally with the pains and the uselessness of existence. But in Heaven a saint is worthier than a man of merely mild virtues, for the saint has labored long and hard in the stony fields of his life and has loved God more than himself, and the lives of his fellow sufferers more than his own. A man who has valiantly struggled with temptation during his lifetime and has contemplated all the worldly delights you have offered him, Lucifer, and has even desperately yearned for them, but who has gloriously resisted you in his soul and in his living, is worthier of more reward in Heaven than a man who has been merely mildly tempted by you or through some accident has not been much tempted at all, or lacked the terrible vitality to sin, or was afraid of the consequences on his own world. The first man is a hero; the second man is one who has had little opportunity to be either a hero or a sinner. Our Father takes note of the human weaknesses of His creatures. He will not permit you to tempt a man beyond his total ability to resist, but He does permit you to tempt His saints more fiercely and more insistently because they are men of greater valor and nobler mind. Our Father, as we have observed before, does not create men equal, but He has established Equity, based on the Natural Law which He ordained Himself. There is no injustice in Him Whom we both love so passionately, and you have never denied your love nor can you destroy it.

Were you the ruler of Heaven the saint and the weaker man would receive equal reward, but that is manifestly unfair. Archangels, who have vaster powers than angels, are more in possession of free will and therefore the temptation to use that will in defiance of God is infinitely higher in degree than in the lesser angels. Archangels are given enormous responsibilities and thrones and crowns throughout the endless universes, because of their nature, and it is they who see the Beatific Vision more frequently than the lesser spirits, and the spirits of men. "To each according to his merits," is the Law of Heaven, whereas on Terra, and other darkened worlds, there appears to be some mangling of the moral law to the effect "to each ac-

cording to his material needs." And that, we know, is infamy, injustice, cruelty, and a display of malice to the
more worthy. Greed is the ugliest of the detestable sins,
for it feeds on its own appetite and is never filled, and its
rapacity is increased by its rapaciousness. It gives rise to
the other sins, envy, theft, sloth, lies, adulteries and murder, and gluttony.

There is happiness in Heaven, as you know, but that
happiness is in degree, except for the knowing that God
loves completely to the extent of an angel's or man's
worth. That happiness is compounded by labor, for none
are idle in Heaven, and there is a task for all. That, too,
is Equity.

While each task is approached with joy and with the
hope—but never the absolute surety—that it will be completed, its completion, when accomplished, leads to
higher tasks, worthy of a tempered spirit. There is always
a progression in the Hierarchy of Heaven. No spirit remains as it was. And, always, there is a possibility, constantly reiterated, that as the spirit retains its free will, it
can will to sin. This is something the theologians, in their
little darkness on their worlds, have never understood or
acknowledged—that there is always the hazard that a
spirit may fall to you, even in the golden light of Heaven.
For God does not remove free will from His creatures, no
matter their degree. If He did so, He would abrogate
their individuality, their very existence, both of which are
eternally precious to Him, for they are of His own Nature
and Essence.

Enough. You know all these matters. You have asked
me if God pursues the lost soul in your hells. That I cannot and will not tell you. Is it possible for the lost to feel
repentance? You have said not—but do you know all
minds?

I am not taunting you, Lucifer, and that you know.

Your brother, Michael

GREETINGS

to my brother, Michael, who believes that he has circumvented me on his new worlds:

No doubt you heard my laughter when I read your letter. Do not be complacent. Damon and Lilith will make their appearances on Pandara in due course, if not to this generation there, then to their sons and daughters. For though this generation may tell their children of what they know, and of what they have seen, and what they have learned, it is in the nature of men to say, "Our parents love legends and tales and strangenesses, but we have not seen the Archangel Michael with our own eyes, nor have wondered at his countenance. Our parents tell us that it was the will of God that he appeared only to our forefathers, but not to us, and that is most peculiar, indeed, for are we not more sophisticated than our fathers, and our daughters more knowledgeable than their mothers? Do we not dwell in cities, whereas they dwelt in the fields and the forests? Have we not learning and understanding, greater than our forebears? Do we not have magnificent temples of wisdom, and do we not stream through the heavens like birds and through the waters like fish, and is there aught we do not know of this world of ours, or are there wonders as yet undiscovered? Are we, then, not wise and therefore more worthy to gaze upon this Archangel Michael, and would we not apprehend his words with more clarity and more subtlety? Why this coyness, that he hides from us—if he exists at all? It is folly. There is no such an archangel, and therefore what our parents have told us has no verity."

You have heard thoughts like these on innumerable

planets, among the worldly children of men who believe they have conquered all things and are capable of comprehending everything. That is my opportunity. For though the generations of Pandara may not yet have fallen, pride in their accomplishments will spur that fall, and pride in their own will will assure their destruction. I will not only send them Damon and Lilith, and say to them, "Do not deny your natural appetites, for all appetite is good, for is it not your nature?" but I will say, "Your parents were simple and mere children in their souls, and had no real will of their own for they were enamored of a fantasy. Have you not failed to discern the reality of Michael in your scientific instruments, and have you found God, of whom your parents speak, in the watches of the night or in your affairs? If there is an angel at all, it is in your capacities, and if there is a God, you are that god, and you must deify yourselves for naught exists in those gigantic universes you catch in your mirrors but your own being. You are the center, the heart, of all mindless creation, and only you have sentience. If you doubt me, show me the proof to the contrary."

That is an argument few men have ever disputed, for the proofs of your existence, and the Existence of Our Father, lie not in the grosser matter but in the towers of the soul. But they will know that I exist! For I will give them delights and conceits and arrogances, and the ecstasy of defying the laws of their fathers, which were the Laws God gave to them. Nothing so exalts a man as rebellion, as we have remarked before, and nothing increases his vanity so much as coming to a wrong conclusion, which he believes is correct. Assure a man that he is wise and knows all things, and that only he exists, and there is no end to his exultant rapture. Even when the men of Pandara become so suddenly aware of the fact that in some strange way death and disease and age and loss have come among them—when once they were absent—they will say, "But this is the inevitable course of nature, and was to be expected! There is a time for living and a time for dying and always it was so, though we have not known it before." You will understand that men have explanations for everything, and the more absurd the more they are accepted. When they discover that the incorruptible has put on corruptibility, the immaculate has become stained, the eternal has become mortal, they will nod their heads solemnly and say, "It is natural—we just had not lived long enough, but time is inexorable. Let us, then, devote our lives to the search for happiness and for personal fulfillment, and not dream as our forebears dreamt, but be courageous men who live that we may die and strive while we can."

They will see my face in their own and will adore me, for am I not the reverie of men, even those not yet fallen?

Why do men prefer to believe there is no God? Is there a fatal flaw even in the unfallen, as it was in me and my angels? You will say that there is, indeed, that "flaw" and you will repeat that it is free will. Nonetheless, men prefer to believe there is no God. God restrains and all chaff at virtue and constraint and the necessity to obey and love. (But many resist the temptation, as you will tediously point out to me. That is beside the argument.) Once God is removed from the belief of men, then they can truly live as they believe the gods live: Enjoying existence, relieved of duty and responsibility, delighting in each hour, acquiring their miserable riches as they will, disobeying even good laws, exulting in violence and bloodshed, exercising power over their fellows—and always for their fellows' own good, you will observe—and committing all vileness in the serene conviction that there is no good and no evil, but only a man's desire and a man's needs. Above all, there is no accounting, for the One who accounts does not exist. So man, they will conclude, is truly free to "live according to his innate nature." All their wars will be holy, all their excesses but an exaggeration of good, all their errors correctable through new laws which they will profusely pass, and all their hatreds righteous. But still there is the inborn, the endowed, craving for perfection, and they will say that man is perfectable.

So they will strive for perfection, which is beyond their earning, and they will seek for merit among the applause of men like themselves, rather than in the smiles of God. They will chase up the mountains of their lives for perfectability, and always there will be the descent on the torrid opposite side, but again they will climb with their banners and their slogans, and always they will fall. They cannot resist the desire for true perfection with which God sadly endowed them—and He cannot withdraw His gift, but they will distort it and in seeking they will never find.

Despair will sit at their right hand and death will dine with them, and decay and grief will be their bed, and sorrow their song, and all that which their darkened souls desired with a hunger that comes from God will never be their own.

And they will descend to me, and will ask again that disgusting question, "If you exist, then God must exist also?" And I will reply as ever, "It does not follow. I am the god you made, and you are mine."

Will the Sacrifice on Terra save these men also? You continually refuse to answer that question, but my curiosity grows with the refusal. In the meantime my hells fatten with the hosts of the damned—who willed their own damnation.

I do not know why I hover so often over Terra, where the immortal Crime was committed—and to what purpose? I watch my legions of demons at work, and I smile at their industry. They hope by pleasing me that I will grant them death and oblivion. You will see that they have much more faith in me than they ever had in God.

Terra is doomed. I watch the progress to annihilation with the only pleasure of which I am capable. Then the memory of the Sacrifice will be obliterated, and there will be no remembrance at all in men, not even of the myth which they declare it is. I will be vindicated, even before His Eyes. He will be forced to admit that I was right and He was wrong. In His second death on Terra the first will be lost, and all men will be mine, even to the farthest planet.

There will be the peace of nothingness, thereafter, and is that not to be desired?

Your brother, Lucifer

GREETINGS

to my brother, Lucifer, who was so roundly defeated recently by a soul of Terra, and who must, despite his angry countenance, be secretly elated:

(Strange how your thoughts hover over Terra, that little world, and cannot be free of her! Yet, it is not strange, for God chose her for His Sacrifice, as we have observed before.)

We have watched, you and I, a certain soul on Terra utterly without merit or Grace for many years, until its flesh was old and scored with living. Even on Terra it is unusual to find so abandoned a soul, so completely faithless, so totally in denial of God and man, so ruthless and depraved. In very childhood, that man was a monster of wickedness and cruelty, though endowed with superior intelligence. In very childhood he was an exploiter of the goodness or innocence of others, and rejoiced in the exploitation. In youth his mind was busy with plots for riches and powers and aggrandizement. He was among the proudest of men, the least faithful, the most cynical, the completely debased. Because of his intelligence and his native gifts, and his magnificent appearance, he found it easy to seduce and betray for his own advantage, and to gather millions of adherents who praised him even while they suffered because of him.

His parents cursed the day of his birth, his wife the hour of their marriage, and his children prayed for his death. Yet never did a man have more devoted friends, for his smile was angelic and his conversation witty and urbane. In short, he was you in miniature, Lucifer, though this remark will enrage and insult you.

The soul had never suffered want or pain or struggle in his earthly existence, had never endured injustice or betrayal or the general sorrows of mankind. Therefore, he was a veritable beast of prey, and his hardness of heart must have astounded even your own demons when they chanced on him. Is it not odd that the soul which has never endured misfortune is the least sympathetic and the least kind?

This man had never once, even in his tenderest years, acknowledged or believed in Our Father, though his parents and his mentors had tried exhaustively to penetrate that alert resistance and to inculcate faith in it. He laughed secretly at their efforts, and despised them, though in his public life he solemnly—and with a laugh in his heart—assured other men of his trust and his belief. Above all things, he was a liar of much genius and accomplishment, and he never spoke truth if he could avoid it or if it could not serve him. Though his parents after their death prayed for him, and though angels and saints when appealed to tried to permeate that adamant and vicious spirit, it seemed hopeless. This man, beloved of his fellowmen, and powerful in public affairs, seemed damned almost more completely than any other soul I have perceived in any world, not to mention Terra.

But he awoke one early morning, and did not know that he was dying. He rose and went to his windows and saw the first light and the first glow of the rising sun. He had seen ten thousand such, and never had he been stirred before. But as he saw the sun touch the height of the trees and the light flow from the sky, he was struck to the heart, and he fell on his old knees and cried aloud, "God, have mercy on me, a sinner!"

What shaft had pierced his soul at last, what revelation of himself and Our Father? You do not know, nor do I. But he threw himself upon the floor and groaned in an awful agony of spirit and hated himself—and believed. He knew penitence such as even few of the just know it —absolute and without question. He lay in his groaning and he wept the first honest tears of his life and said to himself, "Surely I am damned, for I rejected both God and man, and I brought evil where there had been goodness, and darkness where there had been light, and sorrow where there had been joy. I am rich beyond counting, but I am truly a beggar, naked and alone. No man has ever lived more deserving of eternal hell than I, and I shall not regret it but will rejoice in its pains, for it is all I deserve. Yet—God, have mercy on me, a sinner!"

As always, when a soul leaves a body we know it, you and I. But I had heard the anguish of that man's repentance and his plea for mercy, he who had never been merciful, and I arrived beside his dying body as it lay on the floor of his chamber the instant you also arrived. You touched his flesh with your foot and said to me, "He is surely damned." He had fallen there in the brief sleep that precedes death, and I waited.

Then his spirit crept like a larva from the flesh, cringing and wringing its hands and mourning, and the awakened eyes fell upon you and knew you fully, as he had known in life. And he said to you, "Take me, for I am your own, and give me the deepest of your torments, for I am worthy of no more."

But I had heard the Voice of Our Father, and I said to him, "No, you have repented, and not out of fear but out of remorse and a desire to make recompense, and in loathing of yourself. You have asked for mercy, and it is given to you. Arise, and come with me."

He looked upon your terrible grandeur in silence but not in dread, and then he looked at me and shaded his eyes with his hand. "I am not worthy," he said. "If I may be reborn, let me live as the lowest and most contemptible animal, that I may do penance."

Alas, you said to him, "Creature, you have always been that animal, and so I claim you." But you knew he was beyond your power if he so willed. He hesitated, then gazed at me again and I said, "If you will, you can rise and go with me to a place of purging, for you have repented and you need but be made clean of your sins. One died for you, that you might repent your crimes and that you might know Heaven and not death. Accept His Grace and His Sacrifice, and arise."

He stood there, trembling, and he touched my garment and said, "It is white fire, and you have a godlike face, and you must be an angel. Do with me what you will." And he turned from you and departed with me.

You will say that is unjust, and that men far lesser in evil than he live eternally with you in your hells. But Our Father knows true justice. He will never reject the soul that prays for forgiveness and mercy and loathes his own wickedness at last, whether in the morning or the evening of his life. But it must be true repentance, and not out of fear of hell. It must be an awakening of the whole spirit. That soul is now in Purgatory, where he rejoices, knowing that in some hour he will be free to fly to the hands of God, and that he will be assigned tasks of restitution and reparation. He hungers for redeeming labor where once he hungered only for the powers of his world.

When that soul departed with me, I looked back at you and you faintly smiled and saluted me in mocking silence. Were you pleased, Lucifer, that one of your own had finally rejected you in the last moments of his life? You will never tell me. But I hope it is so. I believe it is so, for a single instant light itself touched your forehead and you raised your own eyes to Heaven.

True it is that the men of Pandara, and her sister worlds, may reject God in the future generations and deny Him, and turn to you as their god. We do not know that in surety. Only God knows, for only He sees the future. However, who knows what revelations He will give to those worlds, and what renewal, and what hope for redemption. He has done this ten thousand times ten thousand times over, and will He not do it again? We do not know. I can only hope, and trust in His love.

Doubtless, you now know—for what is there in the planets that you do not know?—that Melina, whose men you persuaded to destroy all their fellows, including themselves, has become, again, a blue garden of the Lord. Between one breath and the next He obliterated the lifeless and enormous cities, which had desecrated the land, and all the vast tangle of huge roads, and the great towers of futile learning and the conceit of statues raised in a spirit of ebullient self-congratulation. All that arrogant man had made in his folly and in his worship of man has blown away in dust, and again the new trees and the forests and the shining fields are merry with animal voices and sparkling with young eyes and gay with the frisking of happy beings. No fear is here, no creatures of prey, no death, no pain or suffering, no storms and terrors. The winds no longer are foul with pollution and fog and filth. The rivers run clean and brilliant, the lakes are like jewels, and the oceans bubble with a new creation. The opalescent mountains glitter in the strong halcyon light that flows from Arcturus, that great sun. There are no gray deserts, which man had made, no scars on the blessed earth, no uglinesses that came from the souls of men. The skies are silent and glowing, for no roar of man-made machines shatter them. The waters laugh, for no ships sail them, and no harbors mangle the shores. There is nothing but rustlings and song and the sweetness of flowered breezes, and long still shadows in the evening and the pure stateliness of the mornings. Melina is a new Eden—awaiting again the lordship of a new race of men, blossoming, fresh with sapphire trees bearing scarlet and yellow fruit, vivid with red grain. All is calmness, peace, happiness, and mirth.

I discern but one thing which gives me apprehension: on a great plain there is a stark crimson peak, lifeless and lonely, like a bleak monument. Is that to be the Forbidden Land, from which men will be warned at the peril of death and their disastrous fall? Our Father, you will remember, always creates an Area of Choice, a challenge to disobedience, a place where men can exercise their immortal privilege of free will. I look upon that peak, and I often hover over it, and I see its terror and its promise of ruin. No living creature approaches it; it appears cursed, in its isolated grandeur. But, when did men ever turn from a curse, at least in so many worlds which we have known?

I cannot ask you, as my brother, not to approach Melina in his beauty, when a new race inhabits him, for if temptation never appears how, then, shall a man exercise his free will? Yes, surely you will tempt the sons of men, however glorious they appear in their new life. I can only hope that they will resist you, that they will turn their adventurous eyes from that ghastly peak, that they will remember the Commandment, and that they will live eternally on Melina in youth, strength, courage, love and Grace, in communion with Our Father, in the smile of their guardian angel, myself.

You have often laughed at me and my guardianship, and have said to me, "You are impotent before me." Yes, it has happened so many tens of thousands of times, and so many times without count I have had to drive men from the Garden and let them suffer their self-ordained fate. Each time I have wept and have said to the sons of men, "Shed not your tears, for you are not victims except of yourselves, and this is the fate you chose, and this is the death you willed, and this is the anguish you invoked, and this is the sorrow you embraced of your own free will. Weep for your children, for the earth is cursed in you, and weep for the innocent beasts of the fields and the mountains and the waters, to which you brought death and ravening hunger and whom you made creatures of prey. Alas, you did this, and not God."

The few six thousands of souls—out of all those billions!—who ascended into Heaven when Melina was destroyed by men, pray for him again and give their blessing on the land and the mountains and the waters. It is they who worked with Our Father to make of Melina the gracious planet he once was, who designed the sunsets and the mornings, who suggested the creatures who live in the trees and the seas, who invented the fruits and the grains. Our Father touched the inventions with life, and He has raised His Hands upon Melina. But only He knows if Melina will fall again under your enticements and your lies. Has He planned, in that event, to give revelations to Melina—as He has done so many multitudes of times before? We do not know. And will the sons of Melina remember, and keep the faith, rejoicing? Or will they spurn the Lord again and again build their monstrous cities of infamy, and their temples of blind learning, and will they again pollute the air and the earth and leave wounded scars where loveliness now exists? I do not know. I only know one thing: there is gold in that fearsome stark monument on the lonely plain. And gold incites wars.

You do not hate me, for you are my brother, and we loved each other in Heaven. You do not hate the other archangels, and angels, who are the guardian spirits of other galaxies and other universes. You would join us—if man did not stand between us, man whom you have never forgiven for having been created.

What you destroy Our Father will re-create. What you lay waste, He will replenish. When you offer death and pride, He will offer life and humility and obedience. When you incite wars, He will strive for peace. You raise up hatred among men, and sometimes the red thunder of it drowns out the Voice of Love, and banishes it.

In the end, Our Father will prevail, and in your secret heart you know it. Why, then, do you strive? Are not the inhabitants of your hells enough for your rapacity? Why would you fatten them the more? Yes, I know all your arguments: Man is an insult to his Creator. Man is unworthy of His Creator. Man, above all, is an outrage to the angels, who must suffer him. Man calls God his Father also, and that is supremely intolerable to you, who love Him with a most terrible and prideful love and would have no human eye gaze upon Him with confidence. Flesh is not that vile, Lucifer, though you believe it is.

Flesh, too, has all the capacities of the angels, for so Our Father willed, and the souls of flesh are immortal. Flesh has its beauties, lesser than ours, to be sure, but still it has charm and tenderness. Man was not created as the angels, except for free will, but when he is majestic and obedient he is not much lower. You would deny God His infinite variety, His smaller creations, His fantasies and His delights. We do not know the meaning of man —but Our Father knows. Yet, like a possessive princely son you would surround Our Father with walls of your own creating, and limit Him to His Throne, and protect

His glory, and you alone, if you had the power, would approach the Holy of Holies, and imprison the King in His own Heaven.

I often wonder: If Our Father had not created man at all would you not have warred upon us, your brothers, to keep us from Him, and hold Him as your own, only? Have you wanted Him as your adored Prisoner? Have you desired the Beatific Vision for yourself alone? As I wrote you before, I saw your ardent and jealous and angry eye when we approached Him, and your hand on your sword, which flashed like lightning even in its scabbard. Would you alone converse with Him, and keep His conversation for your own ear?

He is not the Inmate of His precious Creation! He knew your love for Him, and that is why He mourned you, and Heaven, for a pace, was darkened with His sorrow. He would have you return to Him, in grief and repentance.

How long, O Lucifer, will you deny your own nature and your own longing? Why is life abominable to you?

Your brother, Michael

GREETINGS

to my brother, Michael, who fears for that disgusting Melina, which I cleansed of man, and who believes that he knows my thoughts:

I do not resent that Melina is once more filled with sinless, animal life. Would that it remain so! How beautiful it is, that no man lives upon it yet! It is indeed a garden, fit to be inhabited by angels for their pleasure and their leisure and tranquillity. It is even fairer than before, musical with creation, sweet with innocence, without guile and without pretensions.

But if man is created again for the dominion of Melina, then I shall destroy him through the evil imaginings of his own heart.

You do me an injustice. It is not life I hate, but life that pretends to be like ours. In short, human life. It is that life which I detest, the life of men. Yet, considering, it may be that I do not despise too greatly female human existence, for you will remember that once we looked upon the daughters of men and found them fair, and lay with them and begot sons and daughters of our own. Indeed, as it is written on Terra, there were giants in the earth in those days—flesh of their mothers, essence of ours. Our Father did not forbid that conceiving and begetting. We took upon ourselves a temporary grosser dimension, it is true, but still transcendent, and the daughters of men could not resist us, the lovely treasures! We took them as our wives, and they loved us and bowed before us, and they told their daughters of us, and to this day women dream of us at the side of their husbands. Many of us welcomed the spirits of our wives at Heaven's gate—or at least you more fortunate of my brothers did so.

Ah, women! Would that Our Father had created women only, and not men for them! Imagine all those magnificent planets inhabited only by female flesh, waiting for our embraces! The darling eyes and hair and breasts and thighs of women! I have always loved the female creature. Women naturally adore me, even in hell. They are my most assiduous servitors, in flesh or out of it. They bring the souls of men by the multitude to me. The true laughter in hell is the laughter of women, human or diabolic. With what delicacy they seduce! My own demons cannot spin the lies that women spin, nor invent such delicious delights, not even Lilith. The tender loves can imagine horrors that men cannot imagine, and strange and dainty cruelties, for they are of more imaginative stuff than men. The empresses of Rome, the concubines of Egypt, the Aspasias of Greece, the Borgia ladies—what elegance! Who would not have lain with them, angels or men?

But the women of Terra today are drab wretches, and rare is that loveliness and inventiveness we knew of old, rare that irresistible charm. They vie with men for any office or any condition of life. They are insistent, shrill, grim of countenance, deliberately ugly and contorted, determined that no spot shall be free of them, no employment not their own, no hallowed place unshattered by their peevish voices. It is not enough that they have the power to create beauty and poetry, to bear children, to comfort men, to throw an aura of peace and sanctity about their households. The arts with which God endowed them are now distasteful to them. They would be as men, assuming, against all the Laws of Our Father, the garb of men; they stride like males; they possess muscles. They are fierce and demanding and arrogant, beyond the ferocity, covetousness and belligerence of their men; some now bear arms, they who were endowed with the instinct to nurture and protect life. They go to wars in loathsome uniforms and are proud of their skill with the instruments of death. The tramp of their booted feet is heard in all the cities. They are either imitation men, with men's vices but not their virtues, or they are weak and whining maggots desirous of all things and deserving of none. Now they would invade the very sacred temples, themselves, as priestesses!

Naturally, it was I who offered the lure of masculinity to them. I gave them envy of men and assured them that the masculine world was withholding rights from them, which they eminently deserved, for were they not quicker of wit and more durable? I offered them peculiar lusts and irresponsibilities; I made them despise what had made them women and hold it in low regard. Booted and trousered, they are my own. Unfortunately. I could well endure without these near-men, who come shouting into my hells. The ancient ladies look upon them with horror and say, "What are these creatures, and are they male or female?"

But I owe them gratitude. They emasculate their men and destroy the masculine spirit. They reduce men to the status of cowardly slaves, dependent, desiring little cosinesses and tiny comforts, meager little pleasures and silly consolations. Once the men of Terra were bold and strong and protective, tender with a great strength, delighting in manly pursuits and manly laughter. But now they nestle—there is but one word for it—nestling. They do not guard their houses with the might of their arms, as once they did. No, they brush the hearths and bend over cradles, not to amuse infants or to tease them happily, but to remove excreta and pour milk into their mewling mouths. They wash pots and smooth beds, and, merciful God, they are "companions" to their wives! They are no guardians; they are children, themselves, afraid of their own honest sweat for fear of offending the nostrils of women, or even other men. Their pursuits are feminine, and women have driven them into the designing of garments for their female bodies, or other monstrous occupations.

And women have turned men from them unto other men for pleasures once designed for only between the sexes, and for the procreation of children. It is true that I invented those pleasures, but had men remained men they would not have been tempted by them, and had women remained women their men could not have seduced other men. Yes, it is true that the old Egyptian and Grecian and Roman men turned to their fellows, but only after their women became dominant, their mothers seductive, their daughters manly. I have transformed Terra into a hell where women are no longer cherished or deeply desired, but are feared and exploited in self-defense. Bold and harsh and coarse of flesh and skin, women indeed have changed Terra into a fearsome abode, rife with frightful crimes, ranting with ideologies, and thundering in wars. After all, men have to have some respite from their women, do they not? Craven wretches—I find it in my heart, at times, to pity them.

The women of Terra will destroy civilization as they destroyed it in ancient countries, for nations cannot survive depravity and the reversal of the sexes. Perhaps the holocaust I desire for Terra—and surely it will come soon—is not necessary after all. Meanness and littleness and drabness are a more worthy hell for the men of Terra than universal death—perhaps. Strange, is it not, that it is only the barbarians on Terra who have preserved their masculinity, whereas civilized nations have abandoned it? I muse: Shall I induce the barbarians of Terra to attack the alleged "sophisticated" nations? Perhaps.

I cannot resist Terra! It is so contemptible. One of their beloved sages, a man called Freud, spoke of Terra: "This detestable world." He knew it well, and its vilest lusts, for he was incestuous and prideless, a woman at heart and understanding of women. He hated men, for true men were a goad to him and he despised what he could not be, himself. He now has the companionship of women only, as he desired only the presence of his female relatives.

Do not be tiresome, Michael, and remind me that many women on Terra are still women, loving and nurturing, teaching and sheltering, sacrificing their lives that others might live, and living a life of poetry, reflection, prayer, and faith. They are so few! And they are regarded with scorn by their corrupt sisters and are derided as superstitious or old or backward, or in love with fantasies, or not part of what is called, to my laughter, "this new world."

God gave examples of true femininity to women in the form of holy women, in the shapes of Leah and Rachel and Ruth, and surmounting all others, His own Mother. But do the women of Terra emulate these creatures of Grace, and desire, above all, to be like them? They do not. A woman of gentleness and refinement does not permeate gross politics, nor does she wear masculine garments, nor does she seek sexual pleasures without the inevitable results. She is no toy or a marching "friend" to men, a destroyer of her sons, a destructive and contentious force with her daughters, a shouter in the market place, a contender among males, a heaver at manly games, a muscular monstrosity who is neither male nor female. She is what Solomon said a good wife was, more precious than rubies, and all her ways are pleasantness and all her paths are peace.

Well do I remember Mary, the Queen of Heaven, when she was born and lay in her cradle, unstained by the sin which man incurred at his fall. She opened her infant eyes and looked upon me gravely, and even then she knew what I was. She was not afraid. The light of Our Father lay across her face, and the wings of our brother, Gabriel, protected her. I knew why she had been born; I had known from the beginning. This sweet creature, this frail morsel, this woman, who, even as a babe, was a true woman—Ah, even while I hated her for her destiny, I bowed before her. Hell itself trembled at her birth. She was woman incarnate, the woman Our Father had desired women to be, the image which all women should strive to imitate.

But they do not. A poet of Terra wrote of Mary: "Our tainted nature's solitary boast." But millions of women on Terra scorn her, or doubt that she ever lived, or utter lewd jests of her. I designed it so. Were the women of Terra to become like Mary, my hells would not be fat with female life, and the groves of despair would not echo with female voices.

I turn from the women of Terra with a disgust which even I cannot bear, and look upon the women of other planets, where the race has not fallen, or even where it has fallen. How beautiful are those women, how pleasurable to the sight, how soft of hand, how gentle of speech, how watchful of their children, how devoted to their men! Not all the planets are so, I admit, but none is so ugly as Terra or so base, and Terra deserves her women, and the women deserve the world they made.

And the women of other planets, now destroyed and lifeless, were worthy of their worlds, for it is they who ravished them.

Yes, I know that the fearful stark mountain peak on Melina is filled with gold—and only it possesses that foolish and appalling metal. But I am not committing an error against logic by imputing human, or diabolical, qualities to material of an unsentient existence? Truly, but that is an error men—and demons—commit. Gold is not evil in itself, as Our Father made plain, but only the lust for it. The metal is a beautiful one, intended for decoration and ornament, and a thousand other innocent and pleasurable uses. Nothing is wicked until man makes it so.

It is notable that sparsely settled worlds are industrious and peaceful ones. But worlds heavily populated and filled with infamous cities are the breeding-houses of crime. It seems that men cannot endure the close proximity of other men—and I do not chide them there! I understand it was Our Father's intention that the human female have her breeding season as other female animals have theirs, so that human intelligence would prevent an excess of multiplication and thus an excess of populations, and then, in due course, wars for living space. But when men fell—and still fall—man sinks to bestiality lower than the beasts, and loses all restraint, and with it suffers the loss of instinct and natural rhythms of life, as other animals possess them.

We have discussed all this before through all the tumultuous millennia, and we have observed that with the growth of populations and bloated cities a medium of exchange is necessary to facilitate trade and commerce and the market place—and the inevitable wars. As gold is always the least plentiful of metals, and also the most durable and the most beautiful and desirable, it was natural that it become the medium of exchange among men. In time, it becomes not only the symbol of power but power itself, and that is the greatest of men's desires, even above the desire for women, for with power comes all things. A man may lose his taste for the ladies through age and boredom, but he never loses his taste for the mastery of his fellowman, and this yearning for mastery has its roots in his innate hatred for his brother, born of sin.

Men do not often die for love of God, but they will risk death for the promise of power. And gold is power. The newborn men of Melina will discover the gold in their forbidden mountain, and ennui of ennuis, they will fall again, and the whole wretched story will be repeated. It is fortunate for me that the area of spiritual existence is not confined to material barriers, but can be extended infinitely, otherwise, assuredly, I'd be wanting space for my hells. I will tell the new race on Melina of that wonderful gold in the mountain, and recite them the song of power and the control of their fellows, and the ancient story will be duplicated. I am not immune, sorrowfully, to the sameness of the story, and the wearisomeness of it through the ages.

Man has only to refuse to be tempted, on Melina, to take that gold, but he will take it. You do not know—and neither do I—but sometimes I conjecture if sentience is not a tediousness to Our Father, also, and existence not tiresome. However, when the men of Melina fall again, they will overbreed, they will build their threatening cities, they will desire conquest and worldly glory, all of which rises from the possession of gold. They will deform their world and become a menace to all that lives, including themselves. We are experimenting, in hell, with new weapons of death and fury and annihilation, not only for

Melina but for all the other worlds. One is a simple nega-
tive charge which will obliterate all positive charges, and
thus eliminate not only men but their worlds in one gesture, and set all to floating in harmless gas and mist in the
deeps of space. This is not so dramatic as the crude
weapons I have given to the men of Terra, which can
only set cities to burning to the earth and blinding and
killing and maiming men, and blotting out their breeding
places, and mutating their species. (Ah, it is a fine sight
to see a world wholly burning, like a huge star, itself,
until it is a mere cinder!) But my newest weapon, on
which my scientists are working so avidly in my hells—
their only pleasure that does not ultimately pall—is much
cleaner and there will be naught left of worlds at all, not
even fragments. My scientists are also experimenting with
the negation of magnetic forces and the very laws of gravity, itself. Who knows? It may be within our powers to
destroy all gross and fleshly life everywhere. That will be
my final victory.

You will admit, dear Michael, that I could not do all
this without the fine cooperation of man, and he always
cooperates handsomely. The men on Terra are working
with me enthusiastically, for their own death and the destruction of their planet, and perhaps the rude weapons I
have already given them will be sufficient. They are not
intelligent enough for more lethal and more intricate
weapons, and never will they be, for they are not of the
mind of the dead men of Melina and so many hundreds
of thousands of other planets that were finally cleansed of
human life. My scientists despair of them, and are impatient for their disappearance, for scientists, above all men,
detest intellectual inferiority and mediocrity, both attributes of Terra. Even the earlier races on that dark planet,
before the Flood and the sinking and rising of continents,
were not superior. Yet, in their hatred for their brothers
they need feel no humiliation before other planets, and no
shame or mortification, for they equal the worst.

Well I remember the planet Mercury, in that little solar
system on the borders of your galaxy, Michael, which has
the incredible history of Our Father's sacrifice of His Son.

The ancients were not amiss in calling it quicksilver, for once, indeed, it possessed a cool and argent light, sheltered from the ferocity of the parent sun by thick and perpetual clouds. Small though Mercury is, it once was an exquisite miniature of a world, the illumination pale but shining, its river and lakes pearly and glimmering, its seas dove-colored, its mountains softly glittering, its earth silver-gray with foliage like fragile metal. The clouds that shielded Mercury were the color of dim opals, streaked with rapid and tremulous fire, and the hours of total darkness were short because of the fast rotation of the planet.

The race of men created by Our Father to inhabit that world were as nimble and graceful as their world and full of merriment. They built little cities and cultivated their earth and lived in innocent delight, and created miraculous songs and all the arts in profusion. It did not take me long to plot and consummate their fall and destruction. I told their scientists what they already suspected: that the source of their life was in the hidden sun, and I described other worlds to them, sunlit and vigorous and teeming and possessed of far more color than Mercury, that silvery little world. They needed only to invent a formula to dissipate their eternal clouds, I told them, and they, too, would become a symphony of brilliant hues and tints and shades, hot and splendid and vivifying. Above all, I told them of the majesty of the sun, itself, against which their pale eyes would not be proof, unless protected. And scientists are always eager.

I gave them the formula and the methods to disperse their sheltering clouds from the face of the close sun. You, Michael, told them of their coming destruction if they listened to me, but they said to you, "You would deprive us of knowledge? Are we not men, and was it not designed that as men we should know all things?" I was proud of them, for they spoke in my own language, and with their own words the men of Mercury fell from their innocent state, and Grace, and busied themselves with the works of death.

You will have to acknowledge that it was a notable day

when the scientists began firing their weapons of dispersal at their clouds. The planet was delirious with excitement and expectation. All men ceased their work while they might look at the spectacle. The first effort was not very successful, but successful enough so that the fierce light of the sun shot down upon them for an instant through the torn clouds, and they felt heat and the presence of a radiance they had never known before. It should have been a warning, but naturally it was not. They could speak, thereafter, only of the glimpse they had had of the sun, and the blueness of the sky, at which they marveled. It was a beauty such as they had never dreamed of, but now they dreamt. "Away with these ashen airs!" they cried. "Are we not men, and entitled to the embrace of the passionate sun, and his promise of new life?"

All efforts, thereafter, were concentrated on the total vanquishment of the clouds, and the day came of complete success. I shall never forget it! The clouds coiled upwards like flaming and stricken serpents of fire, and were gone, and the sun poured down upon Mercury unrestricted. The seas immediately boiled; the lakes were gulped in one breath; the rivers sank into the palpitating earth, which dried and cracked and shook and became instantly burning stone. The cities dissolved as if in a furnace, and a furnace it was, before the awful face of the sun. All flesh evaporated at once, and no life endured for more than a second or two. Mercury's orbit, though near the sun, had still been a perfect ellipse; now it was suddenly changed to an erratic orbit, and men live no longer on that blazing little world, one face of which is turned mutely forever on the sun which destroyed it, and which was its punishment. It was a very tragic day, was it not, Michael? But one to be inevitably expected.

No sooner had Mercury become a dead world than out of the darkness moved Venus, out of the far void in which waited other children of the sun for their own experiment in living, and their inexorable death. Venus was so fair a planet, much larger than little Mercury, and when the sun shone on her coldness she came to life, like a dreamer stirring on her couch. Her dull seas became cerulean and warm; her valleys quickened; her lakes sparkled like laughing eyes. Ice fell from her breast, to remain only on her towering mountain heights. Our Father stretched out His Hand and at once Venus seethed with life of endless variety, pink and golden forests, purple steeps, rushing diamond-like cataracts, blue hills, green and yellow grain, fields whispering in balmy winds. Then came the animals of many colors and forms and shapes, vehement with strength and vividness, and with a thousand voices.

Our Father could not refrain. He created man on Venus, as you know, and you visited the first men and gave them, as always, the warning against me, and you called them your brothers and they knelt before you for your blessing. Unfortunate Michael! You smiled upon the aureate heads of the men of Venus, and you looked into their tawny eyes, and you delighted in the sight of their gilded flesh and you rejoiced in the comeliness of the race. Tall they were, as gods, almost as beautiful as the angels, and Our Father had endowed them with great intelligence even in their newborn state. That was a supreme offense to me.

You had told the men of Venus of the vices of concupiscence, and that they must breed only in the ordained seasons, lest their world be overrun and their cities become great hungry mouths of unsatisfied hunger. But again, Our Father gave them the gift of free will. The pleasures of sensuality were permitted only for two weeks every year and at no other time. They knew the Commandment, and for two hundred years they kept it, in spite of Damon and Lilith and all their promises of unrestrained rapture.

Then the younger generations questioned with vexation, "Why should this ecstasy be permitted us only for a brief few days every year, when it is obvious our women are capable of much more, not to speak of ourselves! Why should we be denied? Are we not men, and must we turn our face from our wives and sleep like brothers beside them, until it pleases—whom? Whom are we to please? Oh, our fathers tell us of the Commandment, but we have not heard it, ourselves, nor have we seen this Michael, and we have no knowledge of God but what our fathers have written in their busy books, and what they have preached to us in the little golden temples. But our fathers were apparently men of no vigor and no joy, that they denied themselves in obedience to some myth, and they spoke of 'forbidden pleasures' out of the thickets of their beards. There is no zest in them, no love for experimentation and delight. They withhold themselves from their wives—and in obedience to what, and to whom? Is our race so despicable, then, that we need to limit our numbers? Surely that is defiance of life, itself, and we are lovers of life, and not haters. Let us fill the world with our beautiful kind!

"They say that if we indulge ourselves in our nature—and why should not that nature be indulged?—we shall surely grow old and feeble and die, and our world will die with us. What nonsense! What childishness! Mere pleasure could not bring such calamities upon us, for were we not born of pleasure, ourselves—though only a seasonable pleasure? Let our fathers reveal this Michael to us, and let us hear his voice and the speaking of that alleged Commandment, and let us look upon that God of Whom they talk endlessly."

Are you not tired of the timeless history, Michael, and the same silly words of men? Damon and Lilith were soon successful in the seducing of the Venus race, and in a very few centuries Venus was one huge city and the green land shrank in area and the seas and the waters—a very old story. Wars became more terrible as men fought for places to live and breathe air not polluted by the breaths of their fellows, and hatred replaced all love, even the love of women, and of the gold which they, of course, soon found under my tutelage.

We of the hells came to the rescue of the panting men of Venus. We gave their scientists the secret of inhibiting the breeding powers of "enemy" women, and the secret of the sterilizing of the "enemy" men. What they refused to accomplish as an act of obedience to God they accomplished as an act of disobedience and hatred. I assured the scientists of all the nations that I also had the secret of protecting their own countries—but am I not the father of lies? Children ceased to be born, and as the men of Venus had brought old age, disease, and death to their planet, there was no replenishing of life, no, not even in the shrunken forests and the fields and the filthy waters. Seventy more orbits around the sun, and the race of Venus was no more, and Our Father shrouded the face of the planet with hot clouds, forever and forever.

Then out of the darkness and the void and the cold moved forward the third world, Terra, and Terra quickened and Our Father threw His Shadow of light upon her frozen breast and her dark clouds, and the sun saw the face of another child. Alas.

In anticipation of the coming death of Terra, I have visited the outer planets many times, conjecturing upon them. Mars with his cold red cheeks, Saturn with her rainbowed rings, Jupiter with his huge crimson spot, Neptune, Uranus, Pluto. They do not live, as yet. Are they awaiting the hour when Terra's orbit will be empty and they may move forward into their new places, while Mercury and Venus fall into the sun?

Or, will He indeed, as He promised, come again to Terra? He has said that not even the archangels know that day—and perhaps He has now repented His Word and will not keep it. If He comes as He came before, vulnerable to the wickedness and the plots of men, then assuredly He will die the second death! He will need all the protection of His angels, for never have I seen such a savage and doltish race, no, not ever from the first dawning of light on any of the worlds.

Your brother, Lucifer

GREETINGS

to my brother, Lucifer, who has been very busy of late, and who is the great Plausible, as he will admit, himself:

It is quite true, unfortunately, what it is you say of the women of Terra, but indeed not all. It is true only of those called the "advanced" races where culture is alleged to be the most sophisticated. But, as you have remarked, Terra also has her barbarians, as she always had in the past. I know you are quite capable of loosing the barbarians upon that part of Terra which the people designate as the "West." You have done it before. You did it in Babylonia, in Greece, in China, in Rome, in Egypt, India and other lands of subtle civilizations. You did it on the sunken continents. The signs of your deft seductions are everywhere, while you at the same time inspire the barbarian with envy and greed and yearning for what will kill him, too, when he achieves the state he desires. I agree that man, anywhere, never appears to learn from history and experience.

I, too, have listened to the bold women on Terra and felt my own alarm, where you feel only gratification. They are far worse than their men, whom they have made timid. They do not desire sexual fulfillment for what it was intended, the coming together of profound love between a man and a woman, and the creation of children. No, they insistently proclaim, and in loud and emphatic voices, that they desire sexual experience to enlarge, they say, or develop, their personalities. Their meager, wan, colorless personalities, sunless and juiceless! They do not care for sexual encounters even for the pleasure of them, for there is little substance in them to

90

feel pleasure. (Alas, I am writing almost as you write.) No, sensuality is something to be pursued grimly to "enhance the life experiment and examination." What a most dreary goal! Moreover, they are incapable of the examination of anything, even their own small emotions, and a true experiment would appall them.

But even among these odd and curiously sexless creatures there do live true women, who are aghast at their sisters, though you would dispute the thought. You dismiss virtue as negligible and of no consequence. On the other hand, the vice on Terra seems to me to be particularly pallid and of no originality. Perhaps therein lies the real danger for Terra. Her vice creates apathy or aimless violence. Even the sturdy and unimaginative Romans had more liveliness than the present races, and Greece surpassed them all. Still, there are a multitude of good women in Terra, in hidden places of prayer, in the hospitals, and in the harsh cities. They do not scream for "the full and meaningful and gracious life," as their less intelligent sisters do, for they know that the business of living on that sad little world is in the main sheer drudgery and weary days, with few episodes of bliss and few prolonged excitements. Life, they acknowledge to themselves, is composed of constant little burdens and anxieties and toil and grief and monotonously vanquished hope. They find meaning in their faith, in the carrying of their daily lot, in their service and their love, and they discover graciousness in the wayside flower or in the first rays of the sun on cold brick or stone. They are the true and gentle adventurers, who make of Terra a frequently tolerable planet even for their abandoned and ugly sisters. The merciful love of Mary hovers over such women, for she knows their intrepid character in the face of humdrum living and depressing events. They do their duty, and that is their crown, as faith is their glory. They pray for the peace of simple days, while their trousered sisters stride the streets and bellow. Even the most depraved of Roman women had some beauty, but these do not. Alas, again, I appear to be echoing your own words!

Yes, I well remember your seduction of Mercury and

Venus, and what transpired upon them. Those were days of grief to us—and I suspect, days of grief to you. They were so lovely, far more lovely than Terra. But man and you together destroyed them. In the hours as we count them, and not as men's eons, they will fall into the sun and be consumed.

I have heard men on Terra jeer at the "conspiratorial theory of history." Yet all their history has been conspiracy—between you and them. What other history could there be? Events do not fall upon men; men create them through their governments and their politicians. Terror does not descend upon them from the skies, out of a nothingness. They plot it, themselves. Are not wars always conspired in secret and loosed upon the people with noble slogans, so that they will agree to fight, and die, and not complain? What nation can ever justly claim that it fought a holy war or a war of liberation? History refutes such fantasies. Wars are inevitably fought out of self-imposed fear, hatred, greed for riches, conquest, man-made exultation, or madness. Yet, there has never been a nation on Terra which did not shout that its cause was glorious and just, and that it actually fought for peace and not for war, for liberty and not for slavery. They have cried this through the ages, and they cry it still, and there lies the seed of their universal death. It is you who give them the heroic words that lead to destruction; it is you who arm them. But they deny your existence which, as you have once said, was your greatest triumph among men. Ah, destroyer of men, will they never recognize you for what you are?

My brothers tell me that you are watching Heaven closely of late, to observe our comings and goings. What is it that you fear, or what is it that arouses your curiosity, much more intense than usual? I, too, once saw your shadow fall on the shining battlements of Heaven, and I pondered. Forgive the analogy, but you appear as a great snuffing dog at a shut door, who suspects and dimly snarls, and wonders. I know what it is that you fear, and you know that I know, and you would have me betray some secret in an unguarded moment. If there is some secret,

Lucifer, I shall not tell you. Nor could I, for not even the archangels know.

But I will write of other things, and one is most sorrowful. I have seen your final triumph on Lencia, that mighty and spectacular planet for which I once had such hopes. The race was particularly intelligent and graceful, and inclined to peace. In truth, Lencia had had only one war in her long history, and the very thought of it inspired execrations. Her cities were white and clean, for her universal climate was warm, beneath the benign rays of Betelgeuse, brightest star in the constellation of Orion. Though variable, blazing more fiercely at times than at others, and multiple, his light is golden-scarlet and vivid and fructifying. His kiss can be fierce as well as gentle, and so Our Father created special clouds for those occasions in order to protect the forty daughters of that sun, and their multitude of moons. And Lencia was the largest of those daughters, unfortunate planet, dying child of her father!

From the beginning, even after their fall, the men of Lencia were sincerely concerned with the welfare of their fellows, and this is the reason that Lencia had only one war. As the race was intellectual, though clouded by you, her artists and scientists and architects and engineers designed the most elegant cities I have ever seen, free of filth and pollution. They tended the yellow and crimson and violet countryside with meticulous care, not only for its fruit but to preserve its beauty. Their great pointed mountains flamed with the light of the sun, like torches held to Heaven, and they were the color of bright blood. The seas appeared to be of liquid nacre, fugitive with soft color, and her rivers were brilliant purple. Though the earth was mined for its metals and its oils and its minerals, no scars were permitted to remain, but were screened by lavender trees like huge sprays of feathers, in which grew globed fruits of gold or ivory.

There were no evil spots of gloom or misery or ugliness or decay on Lencia, for the men were industrious and had pride and were revolted by any slight hideousness. All must be harmonious, serene, pleasant to the eye and to the ear, the touch and the taste. The centuries came and departed on Lencia's long orbit about her father, and children were born only when desired, for the men of Lencia were prudent and disciplined themselves. It was hard to believe that Lencia had, in the far past, fallen, for all was so beautiful and melodious, and men were involved in each other.

That was your opportunity. Out of calm you create fury; out of order you create chaos. Yes, it is true that you can do these things only with the anxious and eager participation of man, but still I grieve.

When Lencia fell her sisters were forbidden to visit her, and she was alone among her family, for, fallen, she could corrupt them. Still, it took you many centuries to fulfill your wrath against that great and delightful planet. You did it through the very virtue of the men of Lencia, who still remembered Our Father and did not totally reject Him. But when virtue is carried to excess it becomes an evil thing, and mortally dangerous.

As fallen men are invariably prideful and wish to exalt themselves, you whispered to the more intelligent men of Lencia that they should rule her absolutely, for her own good. It was they who should design her destiny, and control all other men. Lencia had no kings, no emperors; she had only republics, ruled by men who were as just as their fallen nature would allow. But now you inspired a few men with the lust for power, yet they did not call it that. They called it "working, for the common weal, and the expansion of justice for all." They had immense designs, but it was you who invented them. Though Lencia was clean and her air pure, there were still times when the hot light of Betelgeuse heated the cities uncomfortably, and burned the countryside and drained the rivers, though always they were rescued by the clouds of Our Father Who sent rain. But this, said the lusters of Lencia, was a crude and an entirely natural solution. They would control the climate, through the work and designs of their scientists and engineers—but first they must control the people, who might overthrow the plans of their masters-to-be if prematurely informed of them.

The people of Lencia had always been free. They assumed freedom to be a normal state of affairs, and were never troubled at any dream of loss. It was as natural as the air they breathed, and their rulers never spoke of "liberty." It was there. But men of pride come to hate liberty for all—and you told them it was unnatural that their lesser fellows should enjoy what they enjoyed, and with such complacency. Too, humbler men needed their destiny planned for them, instead of living placidly and industriously through their years in a casual fashion. "To what heights can Lencia not aspire, if her future is controlled and ordered!" you said to the men of pride. "And who is worthier to control her than you, great of intellect, seeking only the welfare of your world and your brothers? How they will honor you and bow before you, calling you saviours and heroes and benefactors, and rejoicing in your thrones!"

Fallen men love thrones. It is their ecstasy. Pomp and circumstance are their ultimate desires. Power is their dream. So, they conspired together—with you. Certainly, they had rejected the idea of your existence, but you were the more potent for that. You aroused no suspicion. You gave the lusters of Lencia a slogan for the enslavement of their planet: The Great Destiny. What men are not thrilled at the thought of a unique destiny? The people listened. When the lusters came together the people were notified that mighty schemes were in the process of discussion, and hints were given of incomparable events. The people were excited, and not in the least afraid, though unseen by them I walked among them, whispering warnings. Very few became uneasy, and even those lacked the words to express their unease, for they knew nothing but the climate of freedom. I told them in the dimly anxious midnight that vile, not good, events were about to transpire, and that they should shout the alarm and voice their mistrust. But they lacked the words, and you were careful that they should not hear them at all.

The first act of the destroyers of Lencia was to design and bring to actuality a method to free the cities from the "vagaries of nature." The five billion inhabitants nodded

wisely, though never before had they considered nature
their enemy. But it was their benefactors who had spoken, had they not, and did they not know more than the
man in the street? So the scientists spun vast domes of a
glassy material to enclose the cities and "protect" them
both from rain, and from the heat of the sun. The people
watched their transparent prison rise over their heads and
their tall white buildings, and smiled with satisfaction.
When the storms did come, and the occasional fierce
heat, they laughed with pleasure. For now, under the
domes there was a constant flow of cool dry air, and the
children could play untouched by rain, unscorched by
heat, and unthreatened by lightning. Each man could
come and go without casting a thoughtful eye on the sky.
The climate was controlled.

Only those who tilled the land and tended the animals
lived outside those domes, and as they were not many—
the men of Lencia having invented machines which almost worked the land by themselves—the destroyers did
not fear the few beyond the cities. They knew that men of
the earth are by nature unsuspecting and peaceful, and
not easily dismayed or aroused.

To "protect" the people from disease, said the destroyers, they must never again leave the cities for the countryside, which teemed with "deathly bacteria." They would
live far longer lives, and their children would not die, as
often as they did, of illnesses which were "preventable."
Above all, they must consider their children, who were of
the largest consequence to Lencia. The people amiably
nodded. Their cities held all the amusements necessary
for them, and the streets were lined with trees and there
were magnificent parks and gardens filled with flowers
where they could sit in leisure and peace—under the
glassy domes. The people did not even start or ponder
when guards appeared at the borders of the domes, and
bronze doors were inserted in new, white high walls on
which the domes rested.

So, the people were prisoners. But like all prisoners
they exalted their jailers, and honored them for the "welfare" which they had brought to the citizens of Lencia, in

sedulous love for their health and their lives. Each enormous city had its ten men—the Counselors—and above these powerful ten was the Master, the most profound humanity—lover of them all. When their rulers left the cities it was only on "missions concerned with agriculture, and the greater productivity of the land." The people did not know that their jailers had beautiful palaces in the quiet countryside, where they gathered together to plot further against the innocent, and to enjoy themselves in the free air, and to indulge themselves in new strange vices which you demonstrated to them.

It was so all over Lencia, for destroyers are of one mind. The ships of commerce came to harbors empty of all but those who unloaded and loaded them. The rivers no longer were red with sails of pleasure-seekers, except for the rulers. "It is good; it is charming; it is as it should be," said the jailers. "We alone deserve liberty. We are the Elect, and our children shall marry only among themselves and inherit what we have built for them, and be masters and kings in their turn. And, in turn, the people will bow before our sons and our daughters and obey them meekly, as their fathers do now to us. We shall keep our blood pure from the grossness of our slaves, and we shall be another race, unstained by any weakness of the body or fault of the mind, and in time our very lineaments will be far different from the faces of those we rule."

Liberty is loved only when it is lost. The few on Lencia who had felt uneasy from the beginning, but had had no words, now shouted forth that the world had been betrayed, that freedom was dead, and that the people, if they were to survive as men and not as chained animals, must rise in their might, overthrow their masters and rid themselves of the sterile domes of their happy imprisonment. They must be at liberty to come and go as they willed, and not at the command of the Elect.

But it was too late. The shouters for freedom were seized and quietly killed, for their rulers were always alert for such as these. Their names were given in infamy to the people. They would withhold Lencia's Great Destiny from her. Were not the children safer and did not their numbers increase, and was there not only comfort and quiet and sanctuary and happiness in the cities, and had not disease almost disappeared? Did any pant in the heat, or fear the storms any longer? "It is true," said the people. "The shouters were our enemies." Only their families mourned them, but in fear they did not speak.

Now the rulers moved faster and faster. The people must not be on the streets—for their own good—after a certain hour. There were to be no more elections, even of the Ten, for the supremely wise Masters would choose them. It was a saving of money. There would be no disputations about new laws and so no confusion among the citizens. All would be decided, and planned, for their welfare, in the secret places of the planet. As all must work for the Great Destiny each man's work would be assigned him for life, and he could not leave it. Wiser ones than he would choose what he should do for the benefit of all. The wise desired only peace and plenty, progress and contentment for their people, and they knew best. There would be Councils where the mates of men and women would be chosen for them, "for genetic reasons to improve the race." Marriage would not be permitted without the sanction of the rulers, and the number of children would be decided for each family. The people were a little uncertain about this, and whispered among themselves. They did not know that it was the rulers' intention to permit only the naturally docile and meek and less intelligent among the masses to breed, so that their own positions and the positions of their children would be forever secured.

It needed only a quarter of a century for slavery to be entirely imposed on Lencia. Though I walked among the people in various guises and exhorted them, they were numb and staring at the finality of their fate, which they had brought upon themselves—with your conspiracy. You told them that they were truly free, for nothing menaced them, and that their future had been designed for them and they need have no uncertainties or doubts. They had only to accept their Great Destiny with full hearts of gratitude to enjoy long lives of happiness and work and occasional pleasure. Did not the Masters love them?

Two centuries went by, and it was as the Masters had planned. Their own children did not resemble the children of the people any longer, for their mating had been carefully arranged by their parents to enhance desirable qualities of beauty, strength and intelligence and health. They did not speak the language of the people. In fact, they saw the people only when passing in their closed vehicles to their beauteous estates outside the walls, and they regarded them as animals born only to serve them —which was quite true. And the quality of the people of Lencia declined, and their natures became more simple and brutish, and they had little need of any education, and they died earlier than their Masters for they had been bred out of weakness so that not too many of them would be born, or survive. The Masters had decided on the desirable number of people that Lencia should maintain.

The people were safe. Dutifully, almost silently, they obeyed, and never knew the sweetness of rain or the excitement of storm, and never left their home cities and did not know of the rest of the world—which was as enslaved as themselves. They labored, and enjoyed little of the fruits of their labor; they knew no art. Their entombed cities were antiseptic, and so they never caught the fragrance of winds or felt the heat of the fructifying sun. They were well-kept and comfortable beasts of burden, and that was their punishment. Liberty is the Law of God, and it had been heinously violated.

But you were not satisfied. You thought of wars between the Masters, but they were too content with their lives. You even thought of inspiring rage among the people, but they were too enslaved. What you could not do in three centuries was done for you, out of the very outraged heart of nature, herself.

The people of the planet numbered some five billion. The children of the Elect, and the scientists and artists and professional men who served them, numbered less than two million. As more and more machines were cultivating the land, the countrymen had dwindled to a few thousand, and they were never permitted into the cities. They lived lives as stultefied and as hopeless as did the people of the cities and the towns. No education had been permitted them for three centuries. They, too, had been bred to serve. There was no amusement and recreation for them, and if they looked toward the cities they saw a rounded blaze of glass, sealed away from sound and conjecture. They knew only that the cities devoured their fruits and grains and meat, and that they received, in turn, a handful of silver and a warning stare. They had learned to ask no questions.

But there came a day when the census takers were puzzled. No children had been born on the countryside or in the cities of Lencia for two years, except for the children of the Elect. Another year passed, and another, and another, and the wards of the hospitals where children were born were empty. An investigation was demanded. Who was the criminal who had induced the people not to bear any longer? But there was no criminal, except for nature herself, who could not endure the slavery of a whole planet, where once freedom had lived. No investigator asked himself the momentous question: Can a people become so attenuated and so lifeless and so careless of living that their very reproductive impulses no longer responded? Can life, itself, become so worthless that instinct itself dies? No ruler of any planet has ever asked himself this question, but it is an inexorable one, and explains the death of many civilizations in the universes.

Ten years passed, and save for the children of the Elect, no child was born on Lencia, and another decade passed and the cities and the countryside knew no children's voices. The aged died. The population began to dwindle. The Elect were greatly alarmed. "Who shall our children rule, and who shall serve them, unless the people breed again?" they demanded of each other. The obvious answer never occurred to them. Some thought it may have been the glassy enclosures of the cities, which shut off the sun from the people. Some doctors declared that the imprisoned cities, closed from the sun, lost valuable life-giving rays which may have been the source of the fruitfulness of the reproductive organs. Some suggested that for several hours a day the domes of glass be lifted, in order that the mysterious rays might reach the bodies of the people. But a serious objection was raised to this. If the people scented the wide airs of the world and freedom, who knew but what they would revolt? A little freedom is a dangerous thing, as certain nations on Terra have discovered, and which thousands of other planets have also discovered.

Some there were, among the Elect, who exhorted the people of Lencia to breed, "for the sake of our life and our existence." The people listened, baffled. They did not know why they approached the marital bed so listlessly, and why no encounter brought forth a child. The waters of the cities were then imbued with certain chemicals alleged to stimulate the life-giving properties. The food coming into the cities was instilled with those same chemicals. The people did not breed. Hordes were brought before physicians for examination. The people appeared moderately healthy, though considerably shorter in stature than the Elect, and very docile and meek. It was observed by the doctors that their voices were dull and sluggish, and their eyes uncomprehending, and their bodies flaccid for all their labor. Medicines were prescribed, and warnings were issued by the governments that it would be considered a great crime if the people did not obey. But children were not born, except to the Elect. Hours of work were shortened; more meat was given; intoxicants, denied to the people for three centuries, were suddenly released to them; drugs were issued in mass quantities. The people did not breed. The disgusting anthills where the people dwelt were empty of the sound of children, and people forgot that there had ever been infants. The people aged. It had been designed even before their birth that they would live no longer than the age of fifty orbits around the sun, though the Elect lived one hundred. There were millions of burials but not a single birth except among the Elect.

The rulers gathered together to discuss the frightful situ-

ation, and you were among them, silently laughing. It was
even suggested that the men of the Elect forcibly impreg-
nate the females of the people, so that they would raise
up slaves unto them, for the security of their kingly children. The factories and the countryside were showing the
effects of the dwindling population. Who would serve and
feed and pamper and cosset the children of the Elect of
future generations? Many of the Elect agreed to seize the
younger females of the people for breeding purposes, but
a cry arose: "We must not corrupt and degrade our
imperial blood!" It was a quandary. Nevertheless, it had
to be done, and no doubt you were amused at the alacrity
of the male Elect who went about the cities and the countryside and chose the females with whom to bed from
among the people. The women did not resist, nor their
men. It was of no use. The women did not breed.

Freedom is not divisible. At last, the women of the
Elect did not breed either. The malaise entered into their
bodies and their souls. Desperate measures were resorted
to without avail. The physicians and scientists were
threatened, to their despair. And the population steadily
and implacably dwindled.

Now all are old and decaying on Lencia, and it is a
wilderness. The domes of the cities have long been removed, but the fruitful sun is powerless to stimulate the
life-process. The people did not respond to their sudden
freedom. In truth, they fretfully complained that the rains
wet them, that the sun burned them, that the winds
chilled them, that the lightning frightened them. They implored their masters to protect them again. At last the
Elect learned, too late, that liberty, itself, is a life-giving
force and that men do not tamper with the hearts, souls
and bodies of other men without the inevitable and lethal
result, and that in "protecting" their people from the
forces of nature they condemn them to death. There must
be adversity, struggle, anxiety and uncertainty and hope
in the souls of men if they are to exist at all. The fear of
a dangerous future must constantly spur men on not only
to survive but to live and reproduce and build. If this is
removed then life is removed. Security from storm and fe-

rocity, as you have remarked yourself, Lucifer, is an invitation to extinction. When will the rulers of the planets learn this terrible truth for themselves before the time of correction has passed?

When will your most hated planet, Terra, learn this? Once men are treated as children, deprived of competition and insecurity, and are guarded, they die. It is the law of life.

The thirty-nine sisters of Lencia have studied this phenomenon from afar, and they have pledged each other that freedom will never be restricted from among them. They watch the dying sister planet. Sighing, they await the day when no life but purely animal will exist there, and then they will take the planet for their own, and remember the lesson they have learned.

Or, will they? Will they make a hell of their worlds as so many multitudes have done before them?

Alas for Lencia. If her death will be a warning to all others then she has not died in vain. But men, as you have observed only too truly before, rarely learn from experience and history.

Rejoice, if you will, at the end of Lencia the Beautiful. But, I doubt that you rejoice.

Your brother, Michael

GREETINGS

to my brother, Michael, who himself, alas, never learns from the history of men!

I am sorrowful, not for the death of Lencia the Beautiful, but for your sorrow. You indeed have too tender a heart for the contemptible races! I rejoice, not repine, that again I have proved myself right and Our Father wrong. There are a thousand ways to death and only one way to life, but men indefatigably seek the roads to destruction. If they were not so inclined by their very nature they would not listen to me. Lencia died, not by war, as so many other planets died, but through the sluggish ways of what she designated as peace and security. Again, I only suggested. It was in the power of the men of Lencia to reject.

I am deeply interested in what I perceive of Heaven, where there seems a tremendous coming and going as of late, and not all the faces are joyous. What is it that portends? I remember His prophecy, and so I am alert to any stir in Heaven.

Is it possible that the Christ will degrade Himself again before man on Terra? I shall fight that possibility with all my powers. I shall guard His Majesty. I have already begun the process. Even now, whole nations for the first time in Terra's history are declaring that "God is dead!" This was once the province of only a few cynical and enlightened men, who hardly dared speak abroad for fear of the superstitious and the faithful. Did not Socrates die for something similar, though it was very mild? He spoke of "God" and not gods, and for that he was executed. He was considered a great criminal by the ignorant. Yet he was a man faithful to his noble idea. But the men of Terra, in uncountable millions, are neither wise nor faithful. They proclaim, with their round and defiant faces, "He does not exist!" or "Our old conception of God was wrong and we must have a New Definition!" They even announce that God appears to have vanished from the affairs of men; therefore, He is no longer potent, if ever He was potent. (That, as you know, is my suggestion.)

It is as if ants, who had never seen a man but had heard only rumors of him, declared that as they had not observed him, themselves, he could not possibly live. Other ants had seen the stature of man and had heard the thunder of his step—so they alleged. But as these particular ants had neither seen nor heard the myth was not valid.

To my mind an honest and industrious ant is worth a whole world of men, for the ant labors ceaselessly according to his good instinct, is never slothful, never given to vice or depravity, and as his nature is sound he adheres to it. If an ant said, "There is no Man," I should be inclined to believe him, for ants are sensible, and never lie, and their opinion would be valuable. There are even occasions when I permit myself to dream that there are no men.

My anger is your satisfaction, but as we are brothers I will confess that I am not entirely succeeding in my campaign to have the whole of Terra declare that "God is dead." (But I will!) It was Our Father's design that men should have free will—therefore, that was a surety that He would not interfere. But to my understandable umbrage I no sooner had the millions shouting that "God is dead!" when millions of the lukewarm, in concern, began to examine their consciences and ask themselves, "Is He indeed dead?" Even those who had never believed in Him at all were startled at the thunderous cry of denial, and questioned of their hearts. In all of Terra, now, for the first time in her detestable history, men are not only denying God but are rediscovering Him or finding Him when they had never even sought Him, and should never have begun the search or the inquiry if it had not been for my own damned. Does Our Father believe this is keeping His word that He would never overtly interfere with the will of man? We have always treated each other with courtesy and openness. I find His present and insidious interference offensive and startling. With exasperation and fury I ask myself: Why does He continue to manifest His concern and love for these loathsome creatures, when He has permitted greater and more magnificent planets to will their fulfilled death? This has become an unjust war between two polite warriors. I have not deflected from my course, but it appears that Our Father has, and incomprehensibly. Lay my complaint before Him, Michael, for that is only just.

He will not succeed, though He has already invaded the hearts of millions who never knew Him before and cared nothing as to whether or not He existed. You will say that the extraordinary outcome is my own doing, and not Our Father's, but that is not correct. I feel His presence very keenly on Terra now, and the Shadow of His Spirit.

Therefore, though you swear you have no knowledge of what is truly transpiring in Heaven, I remember the prophecies of His Son, and the prophets, concerning the Last Days when the Christ will come again to Terra and "all things shall be made new." And I also remember that in those days there will be the great calamity which I am devising, and which will destroy man by the hundreds of millions, and his planet with him.

I keep my word, though it appears that Our Father does not. Enough. I will keep my word to make Terra a cinderous mass of fragments between Venus and Mars, as I made fragments of Justia, between Mars and Jupiter. What a glorious day that was, when men on Justia exploded their planet! What a bonfire was lit in the solar system! So fierce was it that the forests of Mars were burned, and the oceans and the rivers seethed and passed away in steam—though men had not as yet lived on him. Uninhabited Terra trembled in her orbit, in the midst of her sullen clouds and ice, and a crimson scar was laid on Jupiter, and Venus, then teeming with men, looked at the skies and said to themselves, "What a wondrous but appalling sight!"

I succeeded in less than one hundred centuries with Justia, whose people were almost as stupid and benighted as the men of Terra. I shall succeed with Terra, also. I am not satisfied with the crude if deadly weapon I have given her men, and the knowledge of which is expanding through my efforts. My scientists are inventing another of vastly more power and destruction. If Our Father continues to interfere, when once He promised not to do so, but to leave man to his own will, then I shall hasten with my plans so that He will look about blazing fragments and on no world at all, and there will be no man to herald the Christ—if He still intends to visit that earth.

But, to lighter matters. We both knew a man on Terra who never in his life ever considered whether or not Our Father existed, and never cared to pursue the matter. I considered him my own. He was not faithless; he was just without faith. Inexplicably, he was also a good man, for all my efforts, just and kind and honorable in all his dealings, merciful and gentle and benign. For reasons I could never understand Our Father did not give him the Grace of Faith, so I was confident of his soul. But when he died he went immediately to Heaven, and Our Father exclaimed, "Welcome, My son!" No, I do not understand.

I thought to amuse you by relating an episode which gratified me greatly.

There was a young man on Terra who possessed a diabolic beauty, but more than that he was an astronomer-physicist of formidable powers, much esteemed in that section called by men the United States of America. (How men love to divide up their planets into sections and give them curious appellations!) Women adored him, but he did not adore them. Proud of his enormous intellect, heaped with honors by his government, a man of many tongues and many minds, he was also blind and did not see what he believed could not exist. In short, despite his intelligence, he was as stupid as his fellowmen.

Eternally unfortunate for him, he had an accident, and in due course he was conducted to my tenebrous palace in the gloomiest section of my hells. I am always fascinated by such men, and infernally piqued by them, and so I received him personally, at my request. I sat upon my pearl and ebony throne, and he was brought to me through the long and murky and silent lines of my demonic courtiers. At the foot of my throne he paused and stared up at me incredulously.

"I am dreaming," he said at last, and then he looked down at his bloodied hands and then touched his bleeding face.

"Indeed," I said with all courtesy. "A dream that never ends."

He turned then and stared at the double line of my courtiers, and they regarded him gravely, the black and scarlet shadow of their wings on the vaulted ceiling of my throne room and on the black and polished walls and on the gleaming dark marble floor. He saw the white glitter of their adamantine faces, the frozen hatred in their illuminated eyes. He shuddered, and returned to me.

"This does not exist," he said. "I am dreaming. I shall soon awaken."

"Never shall you awake again, Man," I replied. "Never shall you sleep again. You have arrived at your eternal home. Do you know me, Michel Edgor?"

"Your voice is familiar." He smiled with that urbanity known only to men of his kind. "I will remember soon. You are very awesome, I must admit, and very beautiful. You are not what I had expected."

"And did you expect me at all?"

He hesitated. "No, I did not. Certainly I am dreaming. You do not exist; you never existed, as God never existed."

I smiled at him, and there was a sudden and sullen roaring in the distance, a clamor that made him flinch. I waited until it had subsided.

"If I existed—and do not, according to you, Man— what name would you give me?"

He hesitated again, and smiled as if at a jest. "I heard of you in my childhood, from my benighted mother and my pastor. That was long years ago."

I was impatient. "My name, Man!"

He was embarrassed. "Lucifer? Satan? Oh, this is absurd! I am talking with a dream."

"It is your dream, not mine, Michel Edgor. You bleed, do you not? That is only your memory of the accident that killed you, on a public road. You do not bleed, in all truth, for souls do not bleed. You stare. You thought you did not possess a soul, did you not? Sorrowfully for you, you do, indeed, and it is your soul which stands before me now. Gaze on your hands again."

He could not take his large dark eyes from me for several moments, then he looked at his hands and started. He felt his own fingers. He said again, "This is absurd. I feel flesh, tangible flesh, yet you assert I am a soul."

"You feel spiritual flesh, and you will understand me when I say it is of a different and more tenuous electrical wave-length than your grosser body, from which you were forcibly ejected only an hour ago, in your time. You will address me, hereafter, as Majesty. Tell me, Man, do you remember your death?"

"I am dreaming," he said, to my weariness. "Yes, I remember I was in a hurry. I was crossing Massachusetts Avenue, in Washington, and I had matters on my mind —and then it happened. I found myself sailing through the air—"

"And then?"

He was smiling once more with that aloof amusement and calm. "Darkness. Majesty," he added, and mockingly bent his knee in a parody of a genuflection. "Then, all at once, I saw a company about me, strange and silent, and I was lying in the street, still and bleeding. Of course, it is all a dream. The street, the white buildings in the sun, the traffic, appeared uncertain as if in a fog, and shifting, and unreal, but the company about me—similar to these I see here now, but smaller—could be seen with greater clarity. They lifted me up, though I was still shaken." He paused. "I saw my body on the street, and the shadows of men gathering about me, and I was taken away against my will. I was brought here. Majesty." He genuflected again.

"And you believe you dream?"

He was offended. "Of course I am dreaming! I am either in my bed or in a hospital. In Washington. Have they drugged me, so that I am having this nightmare? I must have been badly hurt."

"Your body was killed. It was crushed. You died instantly. Your broken flesh lies in a hospital morgue, awaiting the arrival of your one remaining relative, a brother who despises you for what you were, and are. Your body will be cremated, your ashes interred among strangers. But you, yourself, will remain with me forever. I promise you many delights, such as the delicate ones you prefer, and eternal pleasure, if you desire it, or eternal pain, if you desire that. You did enjoy the pleasure of flagellations at the hands of young men like yourself, did you not? My demons will gratify that pleasure, through all the eons without end. You also enjoyed certain dishes and wines. They are yours, throughout eternity. You liked intellectual conversation, and the company of scientists. That, too, is yours. It will please you to encounter scientists of thousands of other worlds, of your own mind, but far more intelligent and intellectual. You will not be restrained by the limits of flesh or time or space, nor any encumbrances. Are you rejoicing?"

"I am dreaming, Majesty." He laughed a little. "There are no other worlds but this. I have said so repeatedly. The earth is the only inhabited planet among a storm of suns and the flow and ebb of universes. I have written books on the matter, to the confusion and disappointment of sentimentalists who would like to believe in an omniscient God, which does not exist, a God of power and glory and endless worlds and galaxies. I admit the galaxies, but never the worlds. The probabilities against them—"

"Are endless. I know, Man. I gave you the words. I always give men the words with which to express their stupidity, their arrogance, their passions, and their desires. They are quite eloquent, as you were eloquent. What was that within you that insisted that your miserable little crumb of dust and mud was the only world inhabited by your race?"

He thought. He was deeply amused. "We are an accident, which could not happen again, unless the exact material conditions existed, and such a probability—"

"Is beyond reason. I am not very intelligent, myself, so I can follow your argument. However, you have not answered my question."

For the first time he appeared uneasy. He glanced again at my silent ranks of courtiers, and a little shudder passed over him. But he is a man not without courage. He said, "It offended me, intellectually, to believe there were others like me on other worlds. I am unique. I stand alone. I am no duplicate, nor are there duplicates of me."

"In short, you are proud. Ah, yes. We share that grand quality together. Let it pass. What did you hear of me on your wretched earth, Man, when you were a child?"

He was again embarrassed, and sought to draw me into his own light laughter. "I heard the myth that you were once the greatest archangel of them all, with powers and dominions, and that you—"

"Yes?"

He coughed. "I feel ridiculous. You—fell. The reason is not very clear."

I said, "I fell for the reason that I objected to your ever existing. I was right. He was wrong."

He was puzzled. "Who is 'he'?"

"The God you have denied all your life, out of your childish sophistication and your idiot's learning."

For the first time a little disbelieving horror came to him. I had not horrified him, but the thought of the existence of God distracted him. Myself he could endure, dream or not. But he could not endure God. As you know, Michael, that is the greatest of hells to my damned: the final realization that Our Father *is*.

He even stammered. "Now I know of a certainty that I am dreaming, either in my bed in my apartment, or in a hospital! For, there is no God."

Again the sullen clamoring rolled over us and he listened and quailed, for it was the thunderous and tortured voices of my demons, who had fallen with me. Even he could not bear it, for it is the most awful sound in all of hell. He put his hands over his ears until it had subsided. Then he said, "Why do they somberly howl like that?"

"Because you deny what they know is truth, and which agonizes them in the remembrance. Do not provoke my demons unduly. They can be very cruel."

But he was pondering and shrinking. "I remember—in my dream. As your—before these dream-images seized me—my instinct was to rise and fly upwards—"

"Certainly. It was the instinct of your soul to fly to the Hands of Him Who created you. It is the deepest instinct of the soul. But you have forfeited your holy right, which was given you at your conception. You are only a man; I pity you. Had I created you I should have been more merciful. I should have granted your extinction on your fleshly death, and eternal sleep and darkness. Therefore, you have the right to curse God, for making your soul immortal. Do so, if you will."

"Curse God?"

"If you will. You will not be the first, nor the last, in the flesh or in the spirit."

"But, He does not—" He halted, for fear of the terrible clamor.

"It is still your privilege to deny. It will surprise you to meet the multitudes who still deny. But they do not deny me any longer."

I rose and my courtiers bowed before me, and the man moved backwards, never taking his eyes from me. "Come," I said. "Walk before me and you shall see."

"I am afraid," he whispered. "For the first time in my life I fear. It is only a dream, but I am terrified. In God's Name, let me wake up!"

"He cannot help you now," I said. "Do not use His Name here. If there is any mercy in you, which I doubt. You had no mercy on your world; it would be strange if you experienced it here."

The thought of any of my souls feeling mercy or pity is my own secret dread. For they are divine emotions, and cannot be countenanced here. It is my haunting fear that they may open a path—but that is incredible.

He did not retreat before me. His eyes were wild. "If you exist—which is not tenable, of course—then He—"

"It does not follow," I said, as I have said millions of times before. "Let us forget Him. You have much to see, and many marvels to discover, in my domain in which you will dwell forever."

It gave me pleasure to conduct him personally through my hells. He blinked in the strong hot light of my beautiful city, and listened to the music and the voices of countless multitudes. He said once, "They do not laugh."

"The only laughter in hell is mine, and my demons," I said.

"Yet, here are all delights, and—I am still dreaming, of course—eternal youth."

"All deliciousnesses. Immortal youth. Souls do not change, nor age, nor suffer disease, nor have bodily needs. You will observe that though light beams here much more brilliantly than ever it beamed on your earth there is no sun, and you cast no shadow. I am the only one in hell who casts a shadow. Observe."

He saw my black shadow on the snowy marble of my streets, and that seemed to affright him more than anything else, but why I do not know. He lifted his eyes to what he believed was the sky, but saw only a blazing whiteness. "There is no night, in Heaven or hell," I said. "In Heaven, there are times of blessed restfulness and quiet and green withdrawals, and contemplations and still bliss. But in hell there is none of that. You were ever a restless creature, from birth, teeming with desires and thoughts and schemes and equations and formulae. I marked you in your cradle as my own. You were never at peace in your heart or your mind. You, like myself, hurried to and fro, ceaselessly. This is your preordained climate, for there is no rest here but only scurryings. You will enjoy it."

He thought he still dreamt. He stood in the heart of my city and studied the sky. "There is no sun, yet it is brighter than noonday," he said.

"It is a light that never fails. It is the light of my spirit," I replied. "Do you not feel it? It scorches, but it does not warm. It illuminates, but it does not enlighten. You will never be free of it, unless you choose my darker realms which men built out of the darkness of their souls."

My multitudes bowed before me as we walked through the city and my heralds trumpeted my coming. The newly arrived soul stared and blinked and observed in utter silence. My damned thought he must be a prince, for it is rare for me to walk with any soul. They gazed at him, questioning, with their lifeless eyes. "They look alike; it is hard to discern any particular feature," said Michel Edgor.

"You, too, have their countenance," I said. "Evil is of one piece."

"I do not know what you mean by evil," he protested, shrinking from the throngs. "There is no good, nor no evil. They are relative terms, and subjective, fitted only to the immediate occasion, need or intention."

"What do you consider evil?" I asked.

He thought. "Ignorance," he said at last.

"But you were the most ignorant of all, Man. You denied the manifest. You looked on the glorious intricacies of nature, and the immutable laws, and you denied the Lawgiver, the Designer. You could have been blind, for all you truly saw of the stars. You could have been deaf, for all you heard of the eternal harmony of creation. The smallest child in his mother's arms knows more about life than you ever did."

"I have done nothing of intentional malice," he said, halting before a vast market place of innumerable treasures, but not really seeing them.

"True. You were too fastidious to be crude. But your very existence was malicious. It was a poison of doubt and despair and cynicism to all who encountered you. You struck the warmth of human hearts cold. It was your intention. You despised all whom you saw, and considered yourself greater than any in intellectual endowments. You condescended. Delicate brutality was always in your voice. Did you ever love? No. The soul that never loves, not even once, is foredoomed. But then, you never inspired love. It is impossible to love an egotist."

He protested. "I marveled, always, at the secrets of nature, which I believed could be, and would be, eventually understood in their entirety. I believed in the coming omniscience of man, and I revered his expanding intellect, his eventual rise to supraman. I worked to that end; I believed in mankind. Is that evil?"

"You will see," I promised him.

"I believed in a secular paradise, which is attainable."

"You will see," I repeated.

He still protested. "You are wrong, Majesty. I did love; I loved mankind."

"But never man. Love of an abstraction is not love. It is only absence of human emotion. Love is personal, not universal, save for One. Come."

I lifted my hand and immediately we were within a city within a city—my very favorite spot, where live and work and dwell all those once famous in their worlds in the arts and sciences and philosophies. My captive looked upon the white and shining towers with amazement, the secluded streets and colonnades which resemble those of ancient Athens, the quiet groups of trees for conversation, the dusky groves of learning, the scentless beds of deadly flowers, the quiet river of Lethe wherein no life moves, but which shines as leaden silver in the noonless light. He saw the men and women walking over the grass and conversing in timbreless voices, their white robes folded meticulously, their faces still as stone. He said, "I understand. Here one can pursue knowledge without the necessity of trying to permeate empty minds, and without the tediousness of encountering obstinate resistance. This is the dream of all men like myself."

"It is your dream," I said. The wandering groups saw me and true emotion glimmered in their eyes and their expressionless faces were filled with despair. They bowed before me but did not approach me. "Why are they not happy?" asked Michel Edgor.

"You will see," I said. I led him into a vast marble hall

filled with exquisite white statues gleaming in the light. They are a forest of stillness, each one more lovely than the last, perfectly executed. Not even Phidias or Praxiteles ever created such. There was no sound but of the chisel and the hammer, where a multitude of sculptors worked. Michel Edgor looked upon these crowding statues with awe, and exclaimed over their perfection and marvelous detail. "What genius!" he exclaimed. "I could wander here forever!"

"You will," I said. I raised my hand and immediately the noise of work ceased, and the sculptors came obediently to me, their heads bent in misery, their hands hanging at their sides. Michel Edgor said to the nearest, "I have seen the greatest in the world, but none so lovely as these! What artists you are!"

The sculptor looked at him with contempt, and another said with disgust, "We can create nothing but what is absolutely faultless. We can commit no error which adds distinction."

Michel Edgor said in bewilderment, "But that is a veritable heaven!"

"No," said the sculptor, "it is veritable hell. Where everything is a masterpiece nothing is a masterpiece, Man of Terra."

Michel Edgor did not comprehend as yet. He stared slowly at the immaculate beauty in stone, and shook his head slightly. Then he said, "You call me 'Man of Terra,' I assume you mean our earth."

The sculptor laughed in derision. "Your earth! I never heard of it until I came to this damned region. I come of a planet far from your own galaxy, which you call the Milky Way, which is only a small and unfathomable and unimportant wisp in our evening skies. My planet, I have learned, is larger than your dim yellow sun, and of an immeasurable loveliness. I was a famous sculptor there."

Michel Edgor was stupefied. Then he said, "You are jesting. There are no other worlds but ours. You speak as our pseudo-scientists, the writers of science-fiction."

The others raised a raucous and mocking cry, save for

but two who had come from Terra, themselves, and they looked ashamed of the new arrival, and hid their faces as if in apology to their fellows.

"You will learn," said the sculptor. They bowed again before me like a white wind, murmured, "Majesty," and left our erudite fool who gazed after them with his mouth open. He began to shiver. He pretended to be interested in nearby statues, then his face fell. "It is a wonderful dream," he murmured. The noise of the chisels and hammers resumed like a taunt.

We entered my picture galleries where my painters work, and the walls are crowded with glowing treasures in golden and silver frames, and the artists plied their brushes and colors in absolute silence, not speaking to each other or aware of each other. Michel Edgor was enchanted. "Not even Raphael or Michelangelo or da Vinci or Rembrandt ever painted like this!" he cried. "What eternal colors, what eternal vistas!"

"They are indeed eternal," I said. "Here, too, no error can be made. Each painting is perfect—and no man's work can be distinguished from another's in style or form or composition or depth of color. No man can say, 'This is my unique creation.' All is as one. No man can excel another. Is this not a wonderful democracy—which you espoused so ardently on Terra?"

But he was studying the painting as if he had not heard me. He stood at many artists' shoulders and watched in silence. There was no faltering in brush stroke, no hesitation. All worked in desperate fever.

"Do you wish to speak to them?" I asked.

He saw their intent and anguished faces, their efforts to make distinct errors or roughnesses. He saw the paint smooth itself out into perfection, as if it had a life of its own, or as if the artist's own earthly desire for perfection prevented him from creating something which could be surpassed by another. He shook his head. "I do not wish to speak to them," he said.

"You should learn nothing, for there is no frustration here," I said. "Is this not truly Heaven?"

I led him to one of my vast concert halls, where musicians were composing and directing their own orchestras. "I hear the most unparalleled executions!" my captive said. "Beethoven was a tyro in comparison."

"True," I said. "You will hear not a single uncertain note, nor a wrong one. These, too, can commit nothing but perfection. All is pure phrasing, pure harmony. Listen. Though many symphonies and concertos are being played they blend into one, with no disruption or clashing. No man can tell his own work from another's. It is as if they played but one composition. Perhaps you can tell me why it gives them no pleasure, and why their countenances are gloomy."

"There is no individuality!" he said, after listening some moments.

"But, is that not what you prescribed, in your egotism, for your fellowmen? Did you not say over and over, in superb confidence to your brother scientists, 'The masses hate and fear individuality, so let us give them sameness and security'? Man, who were you to judge, dismiss and despise other men's souls as if they were not at least as important as your own?"

Now he glanced at me and I saw pure terror in his eyes. He was beginning to understand at last, though he still was not convinced that it was not all a dream.

I took him to enormous laboratories where scientists were testing and theorizing and working with fabulous equipment. His interest came alive again. "On what are they working?" he asked.

"Rubbish," I said. "All their experiments are successful. There are no disputations of ideas. Whatever they invent out of their theories, or prove, is of no consequence. It leads to nothing. There is no excitement about a possible mistake."

"Why, then, do they work with such absorption?"

"What else can they do? They were never concerned, in their mortal lives, with their fellowmen as souls with emotions."

I took him to my endless libraries, whose walls were

tenanted by the damned's millions of books. "Here you will find every philosophy ever tendered by man on any planet," I said. "Here you will find literature as old as time, and history, and conjecture. And you will discover that it means nothing."

"I could spend eternity just browsing here!" he protested.

"You will," I promised him. "And you will be no wiser than before. You will read only perversion and filth and detestation of all that lives, and egoism and blasphemy and the total ignorance which is the true evil. Machiavelli was a child in comparison with the doings of men who lived on other planets. And you will read poetry that has no heaviness, no slightest disharmony; every canto and phrase is perfect. My writers continue to write, and their works are lined here. No one reads them any longer but the newcomers like yourself."

"No one reads for enlightenment?"

I laughed. "They have all the enlightenment, forever, in hell," I said. "They cannot expand their native powers, which were given them at conception. Only in Heaven is intelligence expanded and challenged. Here is fulfillment. Was that not your dream?"

"I am still dreaming," he said. "I am dreaming of Heaven, in which, of course, I do not believe."

"Excellent," I said. "However, one day you will believe, and will realize there is no hope for you. For, you see, no one wins in hell, and no one loses. All are equal in prizes."

"Then, there is no reward for excellence?"

"No."

"If there is no abrasion of ideas, there is no competition."

"True. Is that not delightful? Let me enlighten you a little. Nothing in hell reaches a conclusion, for all is concluded. But would you not call that really Heaven?"

"It is not fair!" he ejaculated.

"But it is most fair. Why should one soul dare to aspire above another? Did you think this was Heaven?"

He stood still in my softly lighted libraries. Then he said, with shamed hesitation, "When I was a child I heard that you were the father of lies."

"Nonsense. Prove it. You see only truth about you here: My truth, which you loved on Terra, and which is rejected by very few."

I led him to my great observatories, full of astronomical instruments and telescopes. He became excited then, gazing about him with eager pleasure as he saw the astronomers with their eyes fixed and intent. "Here is objective truth!" he said.

"Speak to them," I suggested.

He approached one who was gazing through a monster telescope. He said, "I, too, am an astronomer. Can you see the stars from this—place—where there is only light and no darkness?"

The scientist turned to him and said, "Yes. We can see all the universes in eternity, and understand them. Nothing is hidden or left to conjecture."

"Can you see the red spot of Jupiter clearly, and the deserts of Mars and the rings of Saturn and the hot clouds of Venus?"

The astronomer was puzzled, and he smiled vaguely. "What are these of which you speak?"

Michel Edgor became furiously impatient. "Do you call yourself an astronomer? I speak of our solar system."

"And what solar system is that?"

He was confounded. "Ours," he said at last.

"And where is yours?"

He threw up his hands. "You are no scientist! Or you are joking with me."

The astronomer turned to me, frowning. "Majesty, who is this ignorance?"

"He is a soul," I said, "from a tiny little planet about an insignificant sun in the far borders of a galaxy called the Milky Way, of which you have never heard, for it is of the least importance."

The astronomer looked at Michel Edgor with curiosity.

"Then he, too, is of no importance? Yes. What a piteous creature!"

Michel Edgor looked at him umbrageously. "Are you trying to imply that you are a man of an inhabited planet of some other universe? That is ridiculous. There are no other planets like ours, and no other civilized races."

"Be tolerant with him," I said to the astronomer. "He is, indeed, an ignorant soul. Do not be offended."

"I am not offended, Majesty. But you must admit that some souls are beyond toleration."

"You forget. We tolerate everything and everyone here. Tolerance is part of the climate of hell."

Michel Edgor had listened to this exchange in stupefaction. Then he said, "You are trying to denigrate and ridicule me, I who was one of the most important and respected astronomers on earth."

The astronomer was gentle with him. "I know nothing of your earth, soul. I never heard of it. I have never seen it with my instruments. You are a child in knowledge. Come. Look through this telescope."

I knew what he would see: endless inhabited universes, each murmurous with life of its own, and uncountable planets and whirling suns of every color exploding and dying and giving birth to worlds. He adjusted the instrument, and looked, and was silent and rigid as he observed. Then he turned away at last, and sagged.

"I do not believe it," he said. "It is not possible."

"You will believe it, eventually," I told him. "But it will not help you. You will be inspired to worship, but you will not be capable of worshiping."

Will he? That is my dread.

He began to weep and the tears ran down his face. The other astronomers instantly gathered about him, to drink his tears, and he shrank from them in horror. The tears of those who finally confront truth are the elixir of my damned.

I had not done with him, for as he is intelligent he will become one of my assistants in the tedious education of the stupid men of Terra. Nothing so delights the informed damned as telling the newly come of their eternal hell. As we left the observatories and he put up his hand to guard his eyes from my infernal light, he said, as if musing, "If there is evil—"

"But what is evil?" I asked him. "The thwarted, the unsatisfied impulse, the suppression of a desire or an instinct. Is that not what you believed? Here are no thwarted, no unsatisfied, no condemned instincts. You are fortunate to attain everything you wished. This is not possible with the blessed."

"I still believe I am dreaming, and that I shall awake."

"Consider. If, in truth, you will awake in your bed at Terra, what would be your conclusions about this 'dream'?"

He paused. "I might become a different man with a different philosophy."

I laughed. "How uncomfortable that would be, and what derision you would encounter! Rejoice, then, that this fate is denied you. You are safe—with me."

He glanced at me strangely, and I instantly hated him, for I knew he was thinking. Secret thought in hell is very dangerous. I am omnipotent here, but still I do not always know the thoughts of my damned, though Our Father knows all the thoughts of His blessed. This is pure discrimination—against me, and is distinctly undemocratic. I have created a completely democratic realm, but the damned are not always satisfied with their state.

When the Christ was on Terra He said to those who appealed to Him on a dispute with secular law: "I am no divider of men." In short, His Kingdom was not of Terra, and His concern was not with the laws of men. But I am a divider of men; I inspire riots and revolts and rebellions against the law of men and God. I believe I am more just. Shall men be supine, and think only of their lives in eternity? Is that mercy? After all, men are concerned only with their flesh and their appetites—and who should deny them? Not I!

I showed him many more wonders, but he was listless and too thoughtful. Finally I brought him to the Hell of the Wicked Children, whom men, when disturbed by them, call poltergeists.

"But there are no evil children," he said. "There are only evil parents, or stupid ones, or neglectful, or ignorant, or not informed about child psychology."

"There is surely the Hell of the Wicked Children," I told him, and led him there. It is a vast place, full of toys and devilish instruments of self-torture and the torture of others who are weaker. It is a place of malignance and delighted cruelty and destruction and all abominations, far worse, in my opinion, than some of my other hells. Here the evil children play and devise and plot the dismay of others on their former worlds. Children are more inventive than adults, for their imaginations have not been dulled by experience. It is true that they are more gross and violent, but is that not to be admired in an atmosphere of tepidity?

He saw the multitudes of my children in that region, all absorbed with schemes of evil, all gloating with the desire to destroy and alarm and confuse. They are very active. You have noticed, Michael, how active are the wicked, how relentlessly energetic, how tireless. There are no tears in my Hell of the Wicked Children, no repinings, no sad withdrawals. Here is the only applause on invention of some new deviltry. Here is envy of one more intelligent in the devising of an originality. This Hell is not democratic, for here they compete for the accomplishment of terror. They perfect their methods of hurling objects, of barking like dogs, of slamming doors in quiet houses, of howling like werewolves, of casting obscene shadows, of making vile gestures. As they never had any philosophy except the one of confounding adults and inflicting pain on their peers, they are very simple and uncomplicated. I like them the best of my inhabitants. They are truly human.

Michel Edgor looked upon their beautiful and contorted and gay faces, and he recoiled. They surged upon him, plucking at his garments, stamping on his feet, thrusting their fingers into his eyes, squealing, taunting, giggling. He pushed them off, and they gathered again and pinched him or bit him, and he felt the pain and the loathing of them.

"I know you deny sin," I said to him, as he vainly fended off their fiendishness. "But these know all about sin. One could say they invented it. All have been Confirmed in the various ways of their former worlds. Those not yet Confirmed do not come here, for God—pardon me—does not attribute sin to the un-Confirmed. He holds them as saints, incapable of sin. Is that not absurd? I am much more realistic. I would bring man here on his birth."

I directed him to the illusions I have invented for this place: Mirages of animals and birds, for the tormenting of the children. He saw them tear the mirages apart and their delight in the delusion of bleeding and agony. He shuddered. "I was never one of these," he said.

"Ah, yes, you were. You gave your unfortunate mother much sorrow. In Heaven, she prayed for you. But it was all in vain. You possessed your own will. You were never disobedient as a child. However, you agonized your mother with your concealed smiles at her piety, and your soft derision of her teachings. She labored over you, teaching you the precepts of God, giving you all her devotion, for your father died before you were born. You were all she had. She sacrificed her necessities so you could be educated. She believed that you would be a good man."

He faltered, "Does she know? Now?"

This was dangerous territory. I did not want him to think of his mother's prayers in Heaven. I led him away, and he was happy to go with me. I was relieved. Can the prayers of mothers in Heaven help to rescue their children in Hell? This is a thought which continually enrages me, for I have seen some of my more esteemed disappear. I remember the time He descended here—for what reason? We looked at each other, and He smiled. He has said that the "fire is everlasting." But what of those who truly repent? Will you answer me? I know that repentance is impossible in hell—

You will not answer these urgent questions, and this I know.

Your brother, Lucifer

GREETINGS

to my brother, Lucifer, who seems to be losing his temper, which was never of the most patient at its best:

I have indeed laid your complaint of interference before Our Father, and He has said to me, "Remind My son, Lucifer, of the eternal laws of Propulsion and Repulsion. When he enticed the multitudes to declare loudly that I am dead, that was Propulsion, and Propulsion does inevitably, by its very motion, invite Repulsion. As the planets swing in their orbits, by My law, so is a thrust followed by a recoil. He has known this from the beginning. If the lukewarm and indifferent of Terra are asking themselves suddenly anxious and alerted questions, My son, Lucifer himself, caused that reaction though I admit it was not his desire or intention. I rejoice that the indifferent are at last shaken and that they gaze at the skies in sharp inquiry—and I thank My son for giving Me the opportunity to answer. He has created a stir on unfortunate Terra which I have not seen for centuries."

You will discern that Our Father is pleased. Again, the laws of Propulsion and Repulsion have operated, for the loss of Lencia, though grievous to Him, is more easily borne in the light of what you have unwittingly loosed on Terra. Millions of men are repeating your words, "God is dead!" and the next moment they say to themselves, "Is He, indeed?" That very question leads to infinite possibilities, and you can be certain that Our Father will take every advantage of the situation you created!

It is tragic that the very shepherds of Terra are shouting of the Death of God more loudly than their sheep, but this was prophesied, you will remember, by St. Paul,

Dialogues with the Devil   127

himself, and called the Great Apostasy. The shepherds lead their flocks into darkness and confusion and despair, but the darkness and confusion and despair of a soul is Our Father's opportunity. The flocks will repudiate their vainglorious shepherds, and call them anathema, but in all truth they should thank them. They have induced the sheep to shake the wool from their grazing eyes and consider the stars. A great and murky fear has come to the flocks who, for centuries, placidly cropped the grass of Terra and never questioned in their souls and never felt the necessity to question. But, you have posed it!

A truly angelic gesture on the part of the great Archangel, Lucifer! Accept our gratitude. We anticipate that more and more millions will be shaken, and that though they had accepted the Idea of Our Father's existence it was as if animals had vaguely accepted the water they drank without questioning the source, or if the source existed at all. Now they are bewildered, and now they are thinking. Blessed was the day when you received your inspiration! But do not accuse Our Father of inspiring you against your will! He no more interferes with your will than He does with the will of the most insignificant man, and you know that in your heart.

St. John and St. James, the Sons of Thunder, have recently reminded me that when they attempted to induce the Christ to smite fire on the unbelieving towns of Samaria because they rejected Him He refused, and rebuked them. Like you, they now wonder if He regrets that He refrained, and they ask when He will recall His Mercy and strike Terra for her blasphemy and malice. Though saints, they are still men, alas. I recalled to them that they can never foresee the hour which He prophesied, and suggested that rather than hopefully anticipating it they pray for their fellowmen. They were not entirely meek before my suggestion. They are still the Sons of Thunder, and they examine portents with the same eagerness you also examine them, though with entirely different emotions. St. Paul says, "Aha!" before the portents, but he was always an impatient man for all his wisdom. St. Peter smiles benignly; he was always less reckless. He knows that the enslaved lands of Terra hold the thought of Our Father closely and secretly to their hearts, and that they have seen in the wickedness of men, and the cruelty and darkness, the hope of God. The stars never shine so brightly than in the black hour just before dawn—and the enslaved understand that. In the so-called "free" lands of Terra, unfortunately, Our Father is accepted, or rejected, with less passion. Our Father's love operates more keenly in an atmosphere of passionate rejection than in an atmosphere of indifference. For it sets men to wondering, and out of wonder comes revelation, and out of revelation comes adoration.

Again, you have asked me sly questions which I cannot, or will not, answer. How persistent you are! But when was evil not persistent and sleepless? We watch the energetic scurryings of the men of wickedness on Terra, and listen to their vehement voices, and knowing that they are flesh we marvel at their tirelessness. They are all the more filled with ardor because of their pretense—though they seem not to know it is pretense—that they work in behalf of their fellows, and would improve their lot. But we know the evil who guides them, do we not? What arrogance, that they assume they know what is best for their brothers! And with what rage do they greet the resistance of those brothers, who know with all their instinct that madness has now assumed the accents of Love! The more they scream of "Working for mankind!" the more suspicion they arouse. The love of men is always suspect, unless it is first based on the love of God. Indeed, the "secular paradise" which the evil prophesy is a reflection of hell. You will heartily agree.

Men have never needed more than their daily bread, a shelter of minimum comfort, and enough clothing to protect their bodies from the assaults of climate. Their bodily demands are very few, and easily satisfied. But the needs of their souls are boundless, and only Our Father can satisfy them. There is no necessity for ornament, for gold, for large possessions, for downy beds, for treasure. These never content, and those who demand them for all of mankind are fools. They have degraded their brothers to the levels of mindless beasts who want only to fill their bellies and oil their skins and satisfy their animal desires. But man, though soothed with the sweet words of the wicked, instinctively rebels against this degradation. He will eat the unearned bread which is given him, and sleep in the soft bed for which he has not worked, and he will cavort in the stupid, mean little pleasures offered him—but a vast uneasiness grows in the silent places of his spirit, and he says to himself, "Is this all the world holds for me?" Invariably, he has asked, and will again ask, that question, and Our Father waits patiently for the asking.

The young of Terra are, this very hour, asking that desperate question, and are wondering why they were ever born, and to what purpose. They call this wonder "the search for identity." It is indeed a search for what you, and your cohorts on Terra, have denied them. But they will have it! They are turning troubled and thoughtful eyes on the temples which their indifferent fathers raised to God. Man's questions invoke God's answer, and it is always forthcoming. Empty days of happy irresponsibility—which the evil consider a very heaven for mankind—lead to the query: "But must I then die, when I have not really lived? What is this that trembles so hungrily in me, that I am not content? I have no cares and no anxieties, and all is planned and controlled for me. Why am I not happy? There is a longing in me which I cannot explain. But, if I have the longing then there is something which will satisfy me. There is never a question without an answer—and I will search for it."

You have told the young that their mission is to make the future even more desirable than the present for generations yet unborn. But the soul knows that its first responsibility is to itself, and its enlightenment, and its salvation. Though the young indeed do parrot the folly of the wicked—that the generations not yet born are even more important than themselves—they know it is a lie and the knowledge breeds wild discontent in them. For why should they learn and labor when they will never see the conclusion—if any? What is their knowledge worth, and their learning, if it must be smothered in an eternal grave? So, there comes to the young the desire for immortality, that all they have learned shall not be lost.

They know, and observe, that life in flesh is trivial at the worst, and transitory at the best, that there is nothing new under the sun and at the last it is all vanity. Terra is no more man's Kingdom than it was the Christ's. His destiny and the destiny of his children are individually eternal, and not in some far-distant unborn generations who may—if you have your will—not come to birth at all. Nor can any man guarantee what he calls "the good life" to any other man, for man being mortal he is subject to all the agonies of the flesh, of secret thwartings, of illness and decay and age and death, of the inequalities inherent in his very genetic inheritance and intelligence. The years of youth are very few on Terra, roughly from the age of fourteen to the age of twenty-five. Before the first is the dim world of childhood, unformed and not understood. After the latter, age inexorably begins and the responsibilities of existence, and the decline of bodily vigor. Eleven years in seventy, to be young! On that passing moment in time the iniquitous base their argument for the earthly paradise, and many of the young, believing that the handful of years of their youth will be long—instead of the swiftly passing which they are—become the prattling prey of their deceivers.

I have observed that on Terra there is much mad conversation on the "New!" But every age believed it was "new," whereas all is old, all has been tried, all has been discarded, in ages past. The "new" man is as old as Nineveh, and all that he speaks has echoed against the pillars of Rome, the Pyramids of Egypt, the walls of Jerusalem, the purple gates of Athens. There has never been a "new philosophy of man's destiny," for man's mind is limited. You will remember that it was St. Augustine who said that if a man wished to improve the world about him he must make himself a better individual—which is the most gigantic task any man ever faced, and the majority fail in it. For man has to struggle with his nature and subjugate that nature completely to God before he can improve the lot of a single brother.

But who knows this better than you, Lucifer? You detest the man who prays, "Lord, give me the Grace and Gift of Faith, and lead me not into temptation and deliver me from evil. With Your help, alone, I can do my part to make this a better world, a place of more justice and equity, of peace and harmony. Without You I am helpless." You know, Lucifer, the man who prays so will be answered, and in the silence of his own conscience, and his labor thereafter will be gentle and kind and persuasive, and not riotous, violent, and noisy. Love for one's fellows cannot be enforced by any law of the opportunistic and the fools and the hypocrites, no matter how brutal. Not only must man love his brothers because he sees God in them, but those who desire to be loved must also be lovable, and not revolting. Love moves on two paths at the same time, and it is a manly virtue and not the sickly platitudes of the present generations on Terra, who are perverse, and liars.

Man is single, not collective, though ancient and tyrannical philosphies have attempted to enforce the unnatural latter. Man's instinct can never be thwarted except through complete slavery—for which you and your earthly minions are working. It can be temporarily thwarted, but it cannot be killed, no, though generations upon generations of the enslaved may be born. Eventually a day arrives when that instinct reasserts itself, and woe be to your men of iniquity on Terra when again men say to themselves, "I am a man, and my life's years are few on this planet, and without true significance. My destiny is in eternity, through God. My teachers had betrayed me!"

You have raised up an anthropomorphic-centered philosophy called "Humanism," which has declared that man is god, that man's works are of everlasting importance on the planet, that he, himself, is his own saviour. This feeds his pride, especially if he is humble. But inevitably what he sees with his own eyes refutes Humanism: disease, age, death—the inexorable result of the scanty years of living. Especially death. No matter how long physicians labor to increase the span of life of man, the day arrives when he must confront the nothingness of Humanism, the grave and endless silence and darkness. Does he rejoice, in that hour, that "man is all"? I have seen among the blessed, and you have seen among your damned, that man knows in his heart that man, as simply man—no matter how wise, successful, and honored in his lifetime—is nothing. There is no consolation at the hour of death for those who have been denied a more dignified destiny in eternity.

The purse of Humanism is very pretty on its surface, but there is no gold within it. It is flat with intrinsic emptiness. It contains no coin to buy peace at the end of life. It contains no key to anywhere. It is gaudy cloth and ravels in the hand which seized it.

You have spread confusion among even the faithful lately, so that multitudes now question if the Christ ever was born, lived, was crucified and then rose from the dead. And ranks of the stupid—who call themselves wise! —are even declaring that certainly, they accept Christ— but not the Father Who sent Him, and that His Resurrection is only Symbolic. What a dinner of husks you have offered to replace the life-giving Bread! Yes, I know you only offer; it is the will of man to take or reject. The euphoria you have spread among the vociferous, the men of spittle and gesture, who noisily proclaim the Death of Our Father, is the worst madness I have ever observed on Terra, that grievous planet. But, as I have remarked before, you will not succeed. The callow-minded and the little of heart may bow down before you and worship you —though not recognizing you and not knowing you for what you are—but the faithful still live. Their lives will be somewhat less pleasant for what they will be forced to endure at the hands of the arrantly stupid, and they will be subject to ridicule and derision and contempt, and called dreamers or "anti-intellectuals," and they will be accused of refusing "involvement in mankind," and selfish and visionaries, and they will be maligned in multitudinous tongues and despised, and malice will be poured upon them—for do not those who proclaim the loudest that they love their brothers exhibit the most astonishing vindictiveness? But malevolence has the strangest property not only of stiffening resistance to lies and calumnies, but of strengthening faith and resolution. A truly good and faithful man is never crushed by malignance, even if he is murdered, and he stands as a refutation of evil and a light to those who wish to emerge from darkness. His memory may be no more immortal than the forgotten civilizations of Terra, but while he lives, and for a space after his flesh is dead, he has the most profound influence on his fellows.

You may have noticed that the espousers of your doctrine, Humanism, leave nothing at all but a vagueness which is not remembered. If intrinsically good men, they arrive in Purgatory—and great is their astonishment—and more their joy—when they discover that they are wrong! Their deepest regret is that they deprived their followers of the truth, and they confess that they spoke and wrote, not out of viciousness, but out of blindness. But there are others less harmless, as you know, and one was Michel Edgor who sits alone in the fiery dusk of one of your less attractive hells, and asks only for death. He has found the ultimate of what he spoke on earth, in hell, and finds it intolerable.

You will remember that Our Father said that the fool says in his heart there is no God. Terra is now becoming a whole world-wide generation of fools. In that, you have succeeded. Far easier is it for a wicked man to turn from his wickedness, than a fool from his folly, for it is the divine life in man which can eventually make him revolt against evil. But a fool cherishes his foolishness, for it makes him appear, to himself, as of consequence. Pride again is the mightiest of the sins—as who should know it more than you?

It is the fool who proclaims that the Triune God is "not relevant to this century." Consider this century, of which he is so proud! It is the bloodiest of all the centuries of man, the most horrifying, irrational, the most repellent and hating. Its tyrants were not even men of stature and dignity and some grandeur. They have been squeaking dwarfs who can evoke only murder and madness in their fellows. When they speak, and have spoken, of the Manifest Destiny of their nations—and the leadership of the world—it would make angels laugh if they did not weep. No great man has appeared in this century, no man of valor, mercy, glory and tenderness, no man of inspiration. All are little—and the smallest among men are the most proud of their littleness. The century of the Little Man—how repulsive! For the first time in man's murderous history the mediocre has been exalted, the great silenced or rejected. The scientist, who knows only his microscopic speciality, is received as the prophets of old should have been received, but were not. He elaborates on all things, when he leaves his laboratory, yet, if he had any learning at all he would know that he is making one of the most significant errors in logic. Few smile on Terra in these days when a physicist implies that he is an authority on the mind of man. But all nod solemnly when some unstable man, a pseudo-scientist called a psychiatrist, expounds on the meaning of men's dreams and attempts, as men did in Sodom and Gomorrah, to fit all mankind to their neat little beds—and woe to that unfortunate whose head or feet extend beyond the beds!

Alas, this century of which tiny men are so proud! Does it have the splendor of the minds of Greece, and the glory of the law which was Rome? Does it have the scientists of Egypt, the philosophers and the prophets of Israel? Does it have beauty and magnificence and aspiring minds? It stands in dust and war and dinginess, heaped with ugly cities and scarred with the barren wastelands of the stripped earth, its forests felled for the manufacture of trash, its great rivers yoked to yield power and water to crowded and meaningless communities, its silences blasphemed, its retreats and sanctuaries overrun, its countryside howling with drab streets and noxious towns. You and man together—you have done this thing to a world once beautiful and crowned with greenness and fragrance.

You once accused me of a lack of humor, but who can

gaze upon your princedom of Terra, and laugh? Yes, I hear laughter upon it, but it is unmanly or false or childish or bitter, or resembles the raucous cries of apes. I should not, in truth, malign the apes, for they are honest creatures, but you have rid Terra of honesty.

I should not reproach you—for you are the servant of man as well as his prince. You do but his bidding. You and your demons are like the genii whom Solomon imprisoned in bottles and cast into the sea. Man invariably rescues them and the genii obey him. You think I should find this amusing. I find myself sorrowful for you, Lucifer, for you are the victim of your victims.

But even in my sorrow I remember the quiet temples of India, filled with incense. I visit the sad land enslaved by its ferocious Mandarins, and watch men and women and children work silently for fear of their masters, but worshiping in their lonely hearts. I walk among the iron cities darkened by an ancient despotism which dares to call itself new—whereas it is as old as death, and I see the bowed heads of the faithful and watch the secret baptisms of the children, and hear the whispers of devotion in the night. I observe the hot green jungles of Africa and her noble white hills, and though plagued and confused the simple still live there and honor their old gods and consider the wonder of life. I see that all the sanctuaries and retreats and temples have not been destroyed, but remain like islands of light in the increasing gloom of Terra.

A great and good man is as important to Our Father as a great and good world, and there are still some on your earths, and there are bountiful worlds on which your shadow has not yet fallen, or which have rejected you. Recalling this, I can indeed smile, thinking of happier things. In truth, I find considerable humor in this.

Your brother, Michael

GREETINGS

to my brother, Michael, who is as opaque, concerning secrets, as one of Salome's more diaphanous veils:

So, it is true. You see portents in Heaven. Artless Michael, incapable of dissimulation! I thank you humbly. This will give me an opportunity to prepare. Terra is now almost completely mad; the mediocre pride themselves on their intellects; vile little minds speak of "expanding man's consciousness"; the clergy have betrayed the faithful; the dull tyrants sit on thrones; the wise and reasonable and sensible have been silenced; the callow young have been exalted; the haters of their fellows speak loudly of their love for their brothers; freedom is almost extinguished everywhere; the fool is received as a prophet; the mentally illiterate crowd the fora of learning; lawlessness, in the name of "liberty," has banished law; crime has succeeded against responsibility; the depraved and immature demand privileges which they have not earned, but which were earned by their superiors; love is given, not to the worthy who are the saviours of mankind, but to the unworthy; a man is reckoned great on Terra in proportion to his folly; men exult in raising rulers above them who are distinguished not for wisdom and prudence but for their silly "bold and imaginative ideas," which once even children on Terra discarded on the occasion of puberty; truth is despised in favor of lies; facts are abolished in favor of dreams, all of them puerile. There is little virtue left on Terra and even that will soon be driven out. Men shout "Peace!" but they are warmakers in their tiny hearts. They "march for freedom," but they are but troublemakers, overfed with food for which they did not plow, and with money and leisure sweated for by others.

It is a hilarious spectacle. On other worlds, clothed in some fragment of majesty, I have had to contend with the minds of men. But on Terra excellent minds are singularly rare, and so despised. Therefore, I had only to stimulate the glandular systems of Terra's men, and their little bestial instincts, to cause their coming destruction. Once I had more labor on Terra, in the days of Golden Greece, in the sobriety of the Republic of Rome, in the empires of the Egyptians, Chaldeans, Babylonians, Persians, Chinese, in the theocracies of Israel, in the founding of the Republic of America. In short, it was difficult for me in the presence of aristocratic and justly revered minds, in the presence of honor and intelligence.

But mankind, as always, persists in breeding from its worst and basest, and, in the end the worst and the base conceive of themselves as the best and most desirable. That is the very heart of the matter, especially on Terra. I need not destroy her overtly; I can accomplish that through her low-born, so that ultimate chaos will overwhelm that disastrous planet and what civilization she boasts of will revert to barbarism. I can still induce her mad to bring the holocaust on all men. You will discern I have several means of encompassing her death; it is a surfeit of riches. I must consider which to choose. Then, despite "portents" there will be no eye—in the true sense —to gaze on the Christ when He returns, and no ear—in the human sense—to hear His Words. It is a race between us—but I shall win! I almost invariably succeed among men. Terra will be the easiest of all to destroy. I could do it today, but I am fascinated by the spectacle of these ape-like creatures who are now considering themselves gods—as you remarked, yourself. I stand agape at idiots, pronouncing solemnly on the "glorious state of mankind." I am sometimes incredulously mute before the circus of grave imbeciles speaking of the "marvelous destiny of man."

The fault lies with many of the past superior minds on Terra: they did not outbreed the baseborn and the vulgar and the stupid, though it was within their power. They were too gentle and too tolerant of the inferior. They refrained from reproducing, whereas the more apish reproduced in vast and multiplying hordes. They had no strong convictions, for they were dubious even of their own valid conclusions. Therefore, they abdicated to the mindless obstinacy of those who could reach no conclusions at all but the satisfaction of their animal instincts. What was more admirable in man, his rationality, his impulse to worship, his contemplative philosophy, his reverence for art, his passion for the true and beautiful, his awe before creation, his respect for the sanctity of the individual soul, his obedience to the laws of virtue and right conduct, has been obliterated in the vehement passion of the hordes for material gratification. For that, the best will not be held guiltless, I am certain, even by a compassionate God. In truth, I have a multitude of the just in my own domains, who plead that their abdication of responsibility was in the name of "tolerance!"

Innocent Michael! For all your words of hope and mercy there trembles, beneath them, your fear that indeed Terra is lost. Your own indictment of humanity, though written in grief, could have been written by me. At least, we face truth together. Absolute good, or absolute evil: We see things as they are. We have no delusions. It is when men say to themselves: "What is good, what is evil?" that disaster impends. When Pontius Pilate thrust the Christ into the hands of the market rabble—and when did man not do that?—and proclaimed that he had washed his hands of the matter, I sighed with ennui. I have heard the same claim through the endless centuries of Terra. Still, it remains freshly heinous—from your point of view though not from mine. The blurring of good and evil, so that they appear to be in a state of perpetual osmosis, seems to me one of my greatest successes on Terra.

You are wrong in saying that pride is the great sin of Terra, for Terra has no pride now, only servility and the mentality of lick-spittle men. She was never truly proud, save for a very few instances in her contemptible history.

For, I gave men no pride, though some stole it from the angels of heaven. I gave, instead, malice.

The men of Terra embraced malice from the beginning, as we have seen in the case of Cain. Malice pervades the nature of men like a fungus, so that no part of them is clean of the infection. Man sometimes, though rarely, refrains from outright cruelty and barbarism. He never refrains from malice. Sometimes he honestly believes he loves his fellowman, but malice chuckles in his heart even then. Malice giggles before the appearance of justice and honor. It nestles in the breasts of even devoted husbands and wives, and in the breasts of children and parents. It is implicit in the multitudinous laws of every nation of Terra. It flutters like a veil between sworn friendships, however sincere. It lies down with lovers, and rises with them. It whispers below the louder whisper of prayer. It regulates all the affairs of men, and is most evident on solemn faces set in expressions of righteousness. It resides in the judgments of judges; it is rampant between nations. The smallest child delights in it eagerly. When men say they seek justice and the rectifying of injustices, they are inspired by malice to wreak vengeance on their betters. It was malice which hammered the nails into the hands of the Christ.

Malice has stamped its radiant light on the features of almost all men, for malice has a bright and hellish illumination of its own. It is the matrix of all the larger vices of envy and greed and slothfulness and poverty and indolence; it is the inflicter of all pain. It gleams joyously in the eyes of men when they hear of a "beloved" brother's misfortune. It shines vigorously before reports of pestilence and famine and oppression and despair. A man who has given sound advice that has been ignored, and then disaster has predictably appeared, does not say "alas! I grieve with him—or with my people." He says, instead, triumphantly, "I told him—or my people—so! I am vindicated in my perceptive wisdom!" Malice cannot endure superiority of station or of mentality or of Godliness. It must drag it down to its own obscene level, and it demands, at all times, groveling. It can topple thrones or crush a humble, innocent heart. It is the betrayer of betrayers, for though it is never overt, but only covert, it resides in the souls of men from their conception. Before malice even Our Father is helpless. "Who shall fathom the depths of a malicious heart?"

I often think: "Can malice alone destroy Terra?" My answer is yes. Above all other souls in my hells the malicious predominate, for they are liars, blasphemers, abstainers, aggressors, laughers against the good, demolishers of the honorable, murderers in their souls however harmless their acts on the faces of their former worlds. "I never wronged a man deliberately!" millions of them declare to me. "I never lifted a hand against my fellows!" "No," I reply to them, "you did all things under the belief that you were justified; you resented the noble and called them seclusive and of a narrow mind; you envied your brother and derided his successes; you bore false witness against a neighbor and clouded his good name; you scandalized in your mouth to the hurt of those who loved you or trusted you; you imputed depravities to the virginal and the pure; you ascribed unspeakable objectives to acts manifestly good; you believed in no man's honorable intentions and in no man's selfless strivings. You deprecated charity and looked for a mean motive. Altruism, to you, did not exist; it was a concealment for evil. You killed no man and took from him no substance, except that you tried to dim his soul and pretended to scorn his accomplishments. Your wickedness lay in your tongue, if not in your acts. It is the subtlest wickedness of them all, for it cannot be called to account in the courts of men, unlike other crimes."

The few good on Terra are not afraid of disease or cruelty or oppression or misfortune. They stand valorously against all these, facing God. But before malice they are impotent, for it is like a noxious gas which can steal within, undetected, and poison all who breathe it. It is victorious in the sealed house of the virtuous who awake, one morning, to discover themselves overwhelmed. They slept after prayer, but on rising they find a demon in possession, their good name confounded, their reputations blasted, their honor impugned. The doors of their houses are open to all the malice of all men, and there is no refuge. "Who can hide from the malicious man? His works are everywhere, his eye clear and without mist, his ear sharp and keen, his tongue tireless. He believes himself good."

Shall I say to all the nations of Terra: "Unbridle your virile power! The world is yours!" I ponder on that. It is a delicious thought. I contemplate the three contemporary giants of Terra, China, Russia, America. Are they divided by ideology, as they claim? Is their objective kind and true and just? Do they truly wish to invite mercy and peace and plenty to reside with all men? No. No more than other empires are they honorable, no more than others are they bent on peace and tranquillity. They are inspired by malice—no matter their outward acts of compassion—to rule the world. "There is none save God who is good," said the Christ. The malicious are the least good on Terra. (Evil, unlike virtue, is divisible.)

"Let us lead the world to everlasting peace!" the plotters proclaim. But they wish to lead the world only to everlasting subjection to their ambitions.

This is the monstrous little morsel of a world on which the Christ gave up His blameless Life—for what, and for whom? This is the obscure little world on which the prophets lived and whom they exhorted—why? The Law was given this vicious little earth, and it has been despised through the ages, for all of Moses, for all of the Lord. Where malice is king no other thing can flourish, no, not even the bright Shadow of God. Only I can endure.

Michael, my dear brother! I feel sorrow for you. Does it ever come to your mind that the lifting of your hand can blot out this shame of the universe, this Terra? You must ponder on it, for it defames your Galaxy each day it throbs senselessly in its orbit.

My quarrel has never been with Our Father, but with man. Had man not been created I should, even now, have been rejoicing in the courts of Heaven, though often bored by the dissertations of others, alas, even yourself.

Let us speak of merrier things. Congratulate Our Father, in my name, that He appears recently to have improved the human race and its potentialities on the new planet in the Constellation of Orion called Lympia. Has He learned from His previous errors? I meditate on Lympia, a most delectable huge planet as full of color as a brilliant rainbow, its scarlet waters pellucid and calm, its mountains violet, its skies a delicate rose and gilt, its land as cerulean as the dawn. The new human race is delightful to contemplate, shapely and tall and lovely in its form, its skin of polished ebony touched with argent curves and shadows, its eyes as yellow as gold coins, its hair long and black like spun glass, its mouths lifted with laughter and love and tenderness and joy, its touch delicate and sure and gifted, its minds of great superiority and wisdom and subtlety and invention. Among them Phidias and Socrates and Michelangelo would be considered slighter talents. Though they have not existed long they have already raised a wondrous temple of shining silver to Our Father and have decorated it exquisitely. They have paved its floor with midnight marble and its altar is heaped with artifacts so charming that I often pause in admiration. Again, as on all the worlds, the mystic Cross appears above the altars, though few worlds understand what it is and why it is. They only know it has some profound significance. They have but two priests, for they number only one hundred as of this day, but those priests speak in the accents of sanctity and truth and adoration. I observed you only yesterday, Michael, conversing with this tremendously improved race of men, and I saw your smile. Smile, Michael, while you yet have time. It will give me the greatest pleasure to destroy Lympia, or at least the greatest satisfaction. Even this lovely race is not immune from free will—and it is human. Therein is its crime. And I shall punish it.

Our Father has said to the men of Lympia, "You are beauteous, for I have made you, and there is none fairer, no, not in all My worlds and My creation. Not even My angels are sweeter of countenance than you, for all you are only men. Your minds are like scintillating stars, and great achievements are possible for you, to the admiration of other worlds. I have withheld nothing from you, and have given you immortality and free will—the gift above all other gifts, with which I have endowed all My children. This earth is your possession, and on it you will live like gods and angels, free of disease and death, of sorrow and pain. But, you must rejoice in each other, and be proud of the accomplishments of your brothers, and exalt them in My Name. You must delight in your beauty, for I gave it to you. You must delight in your perfection, for it came from My Hand. Degrade these, and all misfortune and death and grief will be your portion."

This is a very subtle prohibition given to the men of Lympia, which could never be understood on such meager worlds as Terra, and many multitudes of others. In each man on Lympia the race is exultant, and the race is exultant in each man. There is no collectivism on Lympia, no trace of that corruption of mind which exists in Terra. There is only joyous brotherhood. But the more ingenious the race the greater challenge to me, and strangely enough my triumph is surer among the more intelligent. There is nothing more satisfying than a worthy antagonist! I find my triumphs on Terra very tedious; they are so easy.

The degradation and deprecation of beauty! That will be a hard task for the men of Lympia, for they are so beautiful. (Beauty never truly existed on Terra, it is the ugliest and dullest of races!)

I will send my Lilith to the men of Lympia, she so snowy of skin, so golden of hair, so translucent of flesh, so blue of eye. She is my Laughing Girl, and what man can resist a woman full of perpetual merriment? I will send my Damon to the women of Lympia, he also so fair of complexion with bright roses in his countenance, and with the deepest red in his hair, and with the dawn in his eyes. You believe that so intelligent and endowed a race will not consider mere bodily beauty, however esteemed, to be paramount over the gifts of the mind? Michael, Michael!! I have yet to discover a human race which did not worship a countenance superior in form and color to others. On stupid Terra, even in Greece and Egypt, a prettier woman was idolized, however vile the soul, and a handsomer man was deified, though possessed of a spirit lower than a worm.

As men cannot look into the souls of others the outward appearance is of the greatest importance. But shall I not speak the truth and say that to all men the external manifestation is the true one? The race of Lympia is not immune to that suggestion. Speech, and writing, even the arts, are not full communication, nor are the whispers of lovers. Man, by his human nature, is forever isolated in his flesh. He can communicate only with words and gestures, with smiles and frowns. He, himself, is hidden from all others. Therefore, he is not understood, except by Our Father, to Whom he rarely has recourse, for the impulses of his natural heart are contorted and naturally perverse.

My sweet Lilith will say to the women of Lympia, "Behold, you are beautiful and beloved of your husbands! But gaze upon my whiteness of flesh, my eyes of blue, my gilded hair. Do not men adore these things? Your husbands have already adored me, for I am distinctive and fairer than you. Your flesh is black, and your hair resembles the dark midnight, and your eyes are yellow. Gather about me, sisters, and I will impart a secret to you so that you will become as I."

To the men of Lympia my Damon shall say, "Look upon my fairness, the brilliant flush of my cheeks, the sunset glow of my hair. Your wives have found all these fascinating. Do you wish them to love you more and forsake me? Listen to me, then, and I will give you the secret of my handsomeness, so that you can improve your race and make your children more desirable, and hence, happier than yourselves."

Do you believe, Michael, that these are trivial arguments to the sons of men? Ah, innocent Michael! You do not understand my Law of Appearances! Before that Law the intellect goes down, ignominiously, even among the intelligent. Men do not seduce gargoyles, nor are women beguiled by dwarfs. The mind is not superior to matter, no, not even on Lympia. Those who will admire Lilith the most will be men of greater sensibility, the artists, sculptors and musicians, to whom beauty is irresistible, and the bearer of it divine. The women who will love Damon will be the ladies of broader imagination than their sisters, and all women love masculine muscles, though they prefer to call it "understanding," and sensitivity.

So, taught by my Lilith, the men of Lympia will become discontented with their wives and cast about them for a woman of lighter skin than their own. She will become the queen among them, the desired dream, the Lovely One, while her darker sister will be considered grosser of soul and body. The women, in their turn, will desire a man who resembles Damon, and will look upon their husbands with distaste, seeking a man of paler countenance. Thus they will commit the sin of which they were warned, and which will lead to their destruction. It will be useless for you to say to the people of Lympia, as you have said, that God has no color, but is a Spirit. By the time I have seduced them they will no longer hear your voice, dear Michael. They will be enamored of what they believe surpasses themselves, and will murmur the virtuous sentiment of "improving the race." For, are they not men of intellect, seeking only the beautiful which is inherent in their nature? The search for beauty has damned more men than the search for power.

Out of what is divine in man I will always cause his fall. I will contrive his hell from his very virtues. What he has not already experienced enchants him, if he is a creature of intelligence and imagination.

I have thought of my demon, Triviality, for Lympia, but the inhabitants thereof would only despise him, whereas he is venerated on such as Terra. "Triviality" is only my name for him; you knew him as Magus, who could, even in Heaven, reduce the profound to fragments, all of them insignificant but all of them ponderous and solemn. He is now the absolute ruler of Terra.

Convey my salutations to Our Father. I find His humor as weighty as yours.

Your brother, Lucifer

GREETINGS

to my brother, Lucifer, who, though he inveighs against
Our Father's sense of humor, has never been able to
make a single man anywhere laugh with joy:

Evil, it has been said, is far more subtle than virtue,
but I doubt it. For one matter, it lacks gaiety, and where
there is no gaiety there can not be true subtlety or variety
or full jesting. In truth, as you have hinted yourself, there
is a certain ponderousness and dullness in evil, as witness
your hells. It can never move lightly, nor with grace,
however beautiful the forms it takes. It can be deadly, but
never can it truly smile. We have forearmed the race of
Lympia and this you would have observed had you not
been so busy with your plotting.

I visited Lympia as I will visit her until a second generation arises. I gathered the lovely black men and women
about me and I asked of them: "Tell me, my brothers
and my sisters, of what color is my substance?"

They rose from their knees at my gesture, and said,
"Your countenance, Lord Michael, is the color of lightning."

I pointed to a crimson rose near at hand and said,
"Should I appear in that hue to you, what should you
say?"

They considered, and then the one they have appointed
as leader to themselves, answered me. "Lord, we should
say, 'He is the color of blood, and therefore his color,
being his own, has its own authenticity and value. It is
different from our color, but neither handsomer nor superior. It is his own, and we honor it, as we honor all differ-
ences.'

"But I am the color of lightning, as you have said. It is the color of my spirit, and your spirits also are of that appearance. God has made man on His many worlds of different refractions of light, and they are a marvel to witness. Some are as golden as your eyes, or your heavens, some are also as black as you, some are red, some have skins of a bluish cast or even a green. But the spirit, as I have told you before, is like unto my appearance to you, and so it is with all men. I come, however, to warn you of a grave danger which the Dragon, as I have called him to you, is plotting for your ruin, your despair, and your agony of mind and soul and body. He will, unto your wives, send you one Lilith, his Laughing Girl."

The women considered this. They laugh merrily and frequently, but now they appeared puzzled. I said, "She is queen of all the Laughing Girls of all the worlds, and she is a serpent. Do not misunderstand me, I do not speak of a merry woman as you know merriment. I speak of a demon, the demon of all the female demons throughout the universe, and she is a demon of wine and roses, of reckless folly, of warm white embraces. She is never serious."

The ladies gazed at me intently. "Life, though we laugh often, is very serious, Lord."

"True," I said. "The keeping of your race and your world is of the utmost consequence and importance. But Lilith, the Laughing Girl, finds nothing of consequence or importance, nor do the women everywhere who resemble her. Her face is never still or grave. She is never in repose. Nor does she say anything of intelligence. Alas," and now I looked at the young men, "the latter men find very adorable in women."

"Not we, Lord!" they exclaimed.

I shook my head. "You are men, after all. Though you are still blameless I am afraid that when your wives are too solemn you find it tedious. Is that not so?"

Their wives looked at them sternly. One young husband then said, while staring down at his feet, "I love the woman God has given me, but she does not always laugh when I do."

"True," I said. "But Lilith will laugh always. She is

never sedate. She was never a matron. Even the women
on the countless worlds who are like her are never truly
matrons, however often they marry. They stretch their
lips in perpetual smiles and show all their glowing teeth
between their red lips; they smile even when they sleep. It
is a bad habit, but it is also dangerous. They are never
disheveled, nor do they ever sweat for they have taught
men to labor for them. They are perfumed at all times,
and their dress is the only matter of gravity to them. Ornament is of the greatest weight. They are never disturbed by the vagaries of nature or of any mishap; they
find it all amusing. Their noses never run, nor, at the
least, visibly. If they possess bowels and bladders, it is as
if they do not. Never are they impatient with men; they
croon and pacify, even when the masculine behavior is
particularly imbecilic of the moment. Good nature at all
times, even under arduous circumstances, and laughter,
always, are their distinguishing features. You will understand that this can be very soothing."

"What trivial creatures!" said the ladies, with scorn.
Again they glanced at their husbands. "Our husbands are
of marvelous intellect, and they would find such women
boring."

I thought to remark that even the wisest men often find
folly delightful, and when it comes in the form of a delectable woman they discover it hard to resist. But the ladies' expressions, when contemplating their husbands,
were thoughtful enough, and appeared to unnerve the
boys.

I said, "God has given you great wisdom, so that you
know things without experience of them. The histories of
many of the worlds is the history of the Laughing Girls,
and the destruction they brought with them. Mighty
thrones fell because of them. Empires died in their pale
hands. Death followed like a lethal shadow behind their
dancing steps. Had fools alone been their prey it might
not have been so terrifying. But the wisest men of all suc-
cumbed to the Laughing Girls, and abandoned honor,
God, peace, and order to lay treasures at their pretty feet.
Their secret, and their charm, is, as I have said, because

they find nothing serious in existence and nothing to be reverenced. They are an abomination, and belong to the Dragon."

"A silly woman is not enticing," said one of the husbands.

"Ah, you have never encountered folly before! Occasional frivolity, or even foolishness, can be very disarming and even innocent at times. But constant folly apparently does not follow the usual course of monotony. It does not pall. On the contrary! I have seen emperors glory in the folly of their Laughing Girls and openly adore them, and turn from them only when they discover the girls in a temper or afflicted with some slight ill of the flesh. I must warn you that it is rare for a Laughing Girl so to display herself to a man, whereas wives, being truly human, lose their amiability occasionally or have to wipe their noses. Men, sad to say, prefer women who are not truly women."

"Do not such women possess souls?" asked one of the ladies in a voice I found a little deplorably sharp. "Are they not aware of this?"

"No, and again that is part of their charm. They are wholly flesh, and their souls are like soft little rabbits, without contemplation or true thought, and possessing only greed. They adore themselves. If they worship, it is only themselves whom they worship. Astonishingly, men find this entrancing. Surely, they say in their hearts, a woman who holds herself above all things and above all other women, holds herself thus because she possesses the truth."

"That she is indeed superior," said a lady. The husbands were curiously quiet, and thinking.

"You have said it, dear sister," I replied. "The Laughing Girls, sly and greedy and rapacious, and desiring all things completely for themselves, teem with plots to satisfy their desires. Men are the satisfiers, the givers of gifts, therefore their basest emotions must be aroused, and their naughtier instincts, and their tendency to abandon. The Laughing Girls, for instance, convince men that they are kings, even if they only plow fields. However, these Girls do not care for the man who labors and who thinks. He is usually not possessed of much worldly substance. So they pursue men of accomplishment, and men of the energy which can gratify greed. Or, men of unusual handsomeness. The latter, however, is only for the hour or the night, unless the handsome man also possesses treasure."

The younger ladies fixed their young husbands with hard eyes, measuring their beauty and they became even more thoughtful. Then one said, "How shall we know this Lilith?"

"Ah! She will appear repulsive to you—but perhaps not to your husbands. Consider this blue lily. Her eyes are of that hue. Consider your gilded sky. Her hair resembles it. And this white anemone; her flesh appears so. Hark to that nightingale, as the evening shadows empurple themselves on your grain. Her voice is like that bird, trilling with music, and, of course, with laughter."

Our Father, foreseeing your arts, Lucifer, has given a measure of innocent vanity to the people of Lympia, so one of the ladies said, "She, from your description, Lord, would appear repulsive to our men!"

"And very strange," echoed some of the husbands.

"The strange woman lives in the house of death and that house is in the habitation of hell," I said. "But that has never driven men from her. On the contrary they have considered her well worth the lives they lost, and the treasure, and their hope of Heaven."

The lads turned their heads and looked over their shining fields to the silver temple they had reared to Our Father. They said with deep passion, "No strange woman can lure us from Him!"

"So be it," I said, and I bowed my head for a moment.

"Nor would we find any woman unlike the glory of our wives captivating," said the boys. "For who is like unto them in face or form, in countenance or in mind? We should spurn this Lilith."

"I hope," I answered. I then said, "But the danger takes another form, and it is of a man." Now every lady regarded me earnestly. "He is a devil, and his name is Damon, and his eyes are the color of the eyes of Lilith, and his flesh resembles hers also, and he has a mane of hair like the vivid sunset. There have been few women who have ever repulsed him."

"How peculiar he must appear!" cried the women with fervency. "How unlike our beloved husbands!"

"True. I trust his color will repel you, my sisters, and that you will not consider it superior to your husbands'. If Lilith is a Laughing Girl, Damon is a laughing boy."

"Life is serious," repeated one of the ladies. "There is a time for mirth, it is true, and life would not be so pleasant without it. But a man who laughs constantly could be an occasion for impatience to a woman."

"True. Women are often wiser than men. But Damon has other arts. He has seen all the wisdom of all the worlds, and all the glories of the intellect, and all the beauty. He can describe them with such vividness that the mind is held enthralled, as if under a spell. He is the father of all the storytellers who have ever lived, all the tales of delight and wonder. Women love storytellers."

"Our wives are busy with the work God has given into their hands!" said one of the husbands in a rebuking voice directed not at me but at his wife.

"Still, they love a man who talks well," I said. "I think that is an art which all husbands should cultivate."

"If he is colored as you have described him, Lord," said one of the wives, "we should find him, not pleasing, but unlike our husbands, and are not our husbands the most splendid in appearance?"

The lads' faces shone with gratification.

"Consider them so always, my sisters," I said. "For when a race comes to believe it is less lovely than another, and that the other possesses more authority and innate value, then it has lost its soul. An honest pride is desirable. A prideless man, or woman, is less than the humblest animal. Cultivate your pride in what God has made you. Should you lose it, and gaze upon the form of Lilith and Damon, and say to yourselves, 'They are fairer than our wives or our husbands, and more interesting,' then surely you have invited death to be your companion, and will bring death to dwell forever on your world. God is good and holy beyond all imaginings, but when what He has created is despised by the created and found of no value, then His wrath is immeasurable. For God has given distinctive worth to all races, and unique qualities, and never must they be demeaned or others regarded with secret envy. Later in your existences and experiences you will meet men of other worlds, and of stranger appearance and color. They, too, have the value of God in them, and it is their own though it is not yours. Love all that is created in the Name of Him Who created it, and know that He does not love one creation above another."

"But will the races on other worlds consider us only unique, or will they believe us lesser than they are?" asked one of the husbands.

"That is an excellent question," I said with approval. "If you do not fall, you will meet only the men of other planets who have not fallen. Therefore, they will regard you with honest admiration and honor God in you. But if you fall, then you will meet sinful men, and you will hate and despise each other, and hold each other in contempt, and you will fall upon each other. And kill."

"We have not seen death," said all of them in horror.

"Not yet. But when you look upon the faces of Lilith and Damon you will see it. Fly from them. Repudiate them. Detest them. Call to God to deliver you from them, and as you are sinless and as you are His, He will come on the wings of lightning to save you."

I believe, Lucifer, that you will find your task of seduction impossible, for the race of Lympia is proud that God has made them as He has, and worship Him for what He has done unto them. They will never, I pray, come to regard themselves as more humble than other races and less worthy of admiration, for they know themselves distinguished and a new invention of Our Father's, and therefore to be regarded with pleasure by others for their beauty of body and mind and soul, and for the greater glory of God. Even if they encounter men of other worlds of superior mind or beauty, they will say to themselves, "It is their own, and we honor it. But ours is our own also, and in the eyes of God of equal value and authority.

If we must strive at all, it must be only to perfect ourselves within the limits of our strength and our spirits."

That is the true humility, and the true Godliness. The race of Lympia knows that they have human limitations, but within those boundaries they will grow to their capacity, and it will be enough in their eyes and in the Eyes of Our Father. For true humility is the noblest of prides, for it accepts itself as ordained by God for His own reasons and His own purposes.

Alas, what you have written of Terra is true, and you and men conspired together to bring it about. Ah, Lucifer! You who so loved beauty to have taught a race of men to love only ugliness! You who are of such grandeur, to have helped reduce a race to such insignificance and so lacking in dignity! You have conferred authority only on the base, for the men of Terra now seem incapable of recognizing baseness. Still a few remain who say with disgust, "I shall not fall before him who rules me, for he possesses no merits of mind and soul, and even his flamboyance, if he has it at all, is bestial. I did not choose him. Therefore, I shall not honor him. I can only regret that my fellowman is cajoled to exalt the lowest and the most inferior, and to raise him above all others. I must strive to make my brothers see, if I die for it, for this world must not perish in mud and blood. It is my mother and I am formed of her flesh, and I love her, and to free her from stupidity is the greatest task to which God had assigned me. I fear no man and no furious nation. I fear only the darkness which man has drawn over the face of God. I will pursue my way, and listen only to my God, and perhaps the children of my children will know grace and freedom and love and worship again. If not, I have still done my best and that will be regarded as merit in me, before God."

In the darkness of the dreadful nights of Terra of this day, these good and saintly men and women remember the prophecies of the prophets and they remember the promises of the Christ. They know Our Father does not lie. His Word is the only Truth, begotten from all eternity. Some, I admit, have been beguiled by you to believe that the material betterment of their fellowmen in secular ways is their task and deserves all their striving. They have forgotten that this world is passing, and that the Christ will make all things new and that the world is not His Kingdom as of yet. They are harried by human impatience for the good, but you have perverted that longing for the good, as you use what is the best in the human soul to betray it and lead it aside. They cry for "Justice!" as they look upon the sufferings of the oppressed everywhere. But justice comes only from God, and if they seek it in the laws of men never shall they find it. Their yearning for universal love and charity comes from the touching passion of their souls, their very instinctual passion, but never can it be accomplished by man's fiat and the exigency in the lustful hearts of politicians. That way leads only to greater slavery. Man puts his faith in mortal princes and rulers to his desperate peril.

It is just that good men cry that all men have a right to the bread of earth, and that intellectual light and earthly peace must not be denied them. But in striving for that bread, that uncertain light and that precarious peace, alone, they have lost the vision. Nothing is permanent on Terra, and tyrants use even benign laws to delude the people and corrupt them. The bread of today becomes the famine of tomorrow, despite all the labor. The light becomes the darkness of cruelty, and the peace becomes war. That is the way of sinful men, of tainted men, of fallen men, even though their work is illusorily selfless and sacrificing. Only through the implored offices of God can they succeed even in a little measure.

Loving and anxious hands must not only give bread, but they must be lifted in prayer and in the knowledge that all secular things pass away on Terra and no morrow is born of today, and no improvement in the temporal lot of man can be lasting until first the favor of God is sought and received, and in the full knowledge that your deathly spirit can only be lifted from the world through God's intervention—as it has been prophesied, and will come to pass on the Day He alone knows.

I look upon the murky chaos and confused terror and hatred of Terra, and the pain and the loss, and I know it is your work, with the aid of men. But it will end! It will end!

Your brother, Michael

GREETINGS

to my brother, Michael, who clothes his dread uncertainty in the pathetic emphasis of certainty:

It will end, on Terra, as I have designed, for Our Father does not oppose the will of man. As I embody men's will, how then can Our Father triumph? The men of Terra have announced their joyous damnation through their governments, and they embrace it eagerly. When the multitudes of them, enfolded with the fire they evoked, look upon my face I shall say to them, "Brothers, welcome to the habitation you have wrought in your lives and in your thoughts and souls, for it is your own. It is surely your own."

Once, less than two hundred years ago, the men on the continent of North America were the architects of a truly magnificent theory of government, based on justice and order and liberty, and in the naïve belief that the majority of men are truly men. It was easy to forecast the absolute failure of that wise government, for men are stupid and prefer to snuggle in the arms of slavery than to stand before the winds of freedom and live arduously. Men, by their nature, prefer to steal than to work, to sleep than to live, to eat than to think, to betray than to be loyal, to dishonor rather than to honor. The evidence of history was before all those selfless and intelligent men who founded the government of North America, but they chose to ignore it. Did they think that by the scratching of their passionate pens they could raise the stature of men by one cubit? They had the words of the Christ: "Who, by taking thought, can add one cubit to his stature?" That which is born in the gutter must return to the gutter, and no efforts of well-born gentlemen will ever elevate a pig to the mind of a man. A dream remains a dream. But reality is the one horror of the gentle-minded. I look upon the twentieth century, as they call it, of the men of Terra, and I know that madness, accompanied by drums, is now sole temporal power all over that disastrous world. It was not I who did that. It was the caressing dreamers who accomplished it, who refused to look upon the nature of man and to deal with it, and therefore evoked insanity in governments and individuals. The truth, as you know, dear Michael, cannot be evaded except at the cost of madness.

But enough of that little foul earth, which lies snugly in my hand, reeking. It is nothing but bloody offal, ready for the sewer it has prepared for itself. I cannot help but congratulate myself, for in this century of Terra I have been supremely successful. It was I who gave the inconsequential gigglers to her, the creators of contorted art-forms, the demented wild "music," the earnestly insistent, the souls who never knew laughter, the anxious watchers of the deportment of others while their own deportment was unspeakable, the enviers, the slothful, the whiners, those who believed life was unfair to them in some vague and petulant manner, the deniers of life, the liars and the dream-spinners, the pursuers of novelty for its own sake, the busy-bodies, the interferers, the philosophers of government who espoused only the vilest members of their society, the teachers of ineffable fallacies, the tolerant of evil who were also the traducers of virtue, the casual and urbane, the planners of the Excellent Society, Hell receive them! and those who believed that filth has its own verity and despised the pure of heart. In short, the unproductive, the twisted, the frenzied and the wild and uncouth. These are my demons, I raised them from my hells to infest Terra and the men thereon received them with love and delight.

My only regret is that my demons did not labor too hard. It was not necessary. There were so few on Terra to challenge them and challenge is necessary to the enjoyment of demons. Strange to say, the little band of the

good and the just look upon the faces of my demons—
and their reflections on the faces of men—and whisper to
themselves, "These do not resemble men in their lineaments and their eyes! They appear to be a New Breed, in
their features and their manners, and a terrible puzzle, for
the earth never knew them before, these distorted creatures!" They are correct. Even Terra never knew them
before, but I am weary of that world and will hasten its
destruction.

I listened with amusement while you harangued the
beautiful black men and women of Lympia. You appealed to their simplest emotions. Have you forgotten
that Our Father gave them superior intelligences? The intelligent are the easiest to seduce, for they can conjure up
a thousand arguments against one question, or in behalf
of it. Intelligence does not always produce steadfastness
and resolution. On the contrary! As it is open to many
conjectures and cannot decide among them, it is filled
with irresolution. And, unfortunately, tolerance.

So, after your last innocent visit to Lympia I appeared
to the busy inhabitants, and they looked upon me startled. I smiled at them, and they became uncertain. Then a
young man said to me, "You have the appearance and
color of lightning, and your eyes are blue like the eyes of
the Lord Michael, the archangel who protects and guides
us. Your hair is as black as ours, but you have the stature
and the heroic appearance of an archangel, and you are
most grand and beautiful. Who are you?"

I said, still smiling, "I am he whom Michael calls the
Dragon. Tell me. Am I so formidable and hateful in appearance, so detestable and loathsome, that you must
turn from me in disgust?"

The ladies, bless them, replied, "No, you are splendid
beyond imagining."

I said, "I am he whom God called His Star of the
Morning. I am indeed an archangel, and I am the most
powerful of them all, for God gave me my power, and I
stood at His hand and He loved me."

"Then," said one lad with dubiousness, "you are good
and not evil?"

"That is purely a matter of opinion," I answered. "It is also a subjective matter. The question has no place in the realm of reality."

It is delicious to converse with an intelligent race.

"The Lord Michael has warned us against you," said a young husband, gazing at me with fear, and retreating. But I smiled superbly.

"Michael is my dearly beloved brother," I said. "He is younger, in time, than I. I was created before him, by God, Whom you honor. There is none dearer to my heart than Michael, save Our Father."

The intelligent are always seduced by a reasonable manner and a reasonable argument, and especially when one appears to agree with them. So the men, and ladies, of Lympia approached me nearer and looked upon me, enchanted. The ladies were particularly charmed; they cannot resist masculine beauty. I gazed slowly and admiringly about their lovely world and sighed as if rapturous. "What infinite possibilities are here!" I exclaimed.

One young man said to me doubtfully, "We have been warned to hold no conversation with you, Lucifer."

"Oh, come," I said with indulgence. "Are you witless children? Your lord, Michael, does not appreciate your intellect, for he is afraid of intellect in men. He would prefer that you remain infants, unable to order your own destiny, and enhance the effulgence of your remarkable world. Do you wish to exist in a garden all your lives, or would you be glorious, beyond all the other races of men on all the other worlds?"

As you have said, Michael, Our Father gave the men of Lympia some innocent vanity, and it was through this gift that I approached them.

"It will not be a small garden perpetually," said one young man. "We shall create cities of stupendous beauty and grandeur, filled with light and music and happiness and joy and the knowledge of God. Our children will inhabit those cities, and their children's children, and we will contemplate them and give adoration to God, Who ordained it all."

"That is quite true," I replied. "Nothing in all the endless universes will surpass Lympia, if you are willing to accept my help. I love beauty above all things. I love intellect, which, alas, Michael does not. Who can resist you, men of Lympia, who will soon have the means to soar among all the worlds, and give them the fruits of your knowledge? It is your duty; surely, it is your duty! There are multitudes of worlds which dwell in darkness and ignorance and are low in mentality. You will bring to them the mightiness of your minds, your inventions, your insights, your magnificent instincts for majesty and loveliness, your innate passions for art and wisdom and philosophy. Is not Lympia your mother and your joy? How is it possible for you to deny other worlds what your world possesses? Is that not the ultimate in selfishness and disregard for the souls of others?"

They pondered, uneasily. Then I raised my hand and in the golden skies there appeared before them the image of Terra, and I let them dwell for a space on the horrors of that repulsive world. They stared, shrinking and incredulous. I permitted them to listen to the clamor of the mad voices, the clashes of arms, the stupid and intense faces of the leaders, their wild eyes and disordered gestures. I let them study the governments.

Then they cried out, shuddering, and hiding their faces in their hands. "It does not exist! It cannot exist! Such fury and bestiality cannot be in the universe!"

"Unfortunately," I said, "you have gazed on reality, not only on that tiny world, but on countless other worlds. Does it not move your hearts to compassion, and to the question: 'Why does God permit such nightmares?' "

One young man dropped his hands slowly, and his eyes were dilated with the dreadfulness of what he had contemplated. "Indeed," he said, "why does Our Father permit it?"

"To be honest," I said, "they chose it for themselves. They were created inferior and debased, but why I do not know. Only God can answer that question. Tell me. Has not Michael already told you that it is your duty to increase your race and your accomplishments?"

"True," said one lady. She was sweating with anxiety,

but I noticed with satisfaction that she concealed her sweat from her husband! I thank you, Michael.

"How, then, can you increase your race and your accomplishments? By working ceaselessly. But it is your duty to displace ugliness with beauty, darkness with light, stupidity with wisdom, among all the worlds. Are not your hearts moved by what you have seen? Can you be so cruel as to deny other worlds what you already possess? That is intellectual arrogance, and there is nothing that is so despised by God. Yes, I know that God gave you your intellects. But does He wish that you hold them to yourselves, only? If He made you so, is it not His desire that you give your gifts to others? As you are blessed, are you not worthy to rule other worlds in sanity, justice, peace, grace and enlightenment and happiness?

"You must remember that God has millions of universes. He has endowed some of His worlds with superior souls and minds. Does He expect that you remain idle? No! It is surely His will that you help to improve the grosser worlds." I paused. "And rule them," I added in the softest voice. "Surely if you consider a moment, you will know that is God's intention."

"It is true that we are superior to what we have seen of that world you have shown us," said a young man. "Those men, if they be truly men, are like beasts."

"They are indeed beasts, alas. They have no inspirations. They create no beauty nor splendor. Their voices are like crows; their souls are steeped in error. They wander like mindless sheep, but violent sheep. You have seen only one of these deplorable worlds, ready for your leadership and your intellects. Did you study their ugliness of body, their meanness of feature? You can, with my help, bring sanity to them and nobler stature and grace. Are not your hearts moved to do this?"

"Are you suggesting that when we visit them we must interbreed with them?" asked a girl with loathing.

"You are beautiful. Is it wrong to raise up these monstrous races and give them your countenances, and your marvelous bodies? Is it to be accounted sinful to lead them with your minds? You have seen their architecture, which is a nightmare in itself. Look upon the temple you have built to God, perfect in all its lines and radiance. Is it not wicked to withhold your arts from other races? You are superior; you are like gods, yourselves. The burden will be heavy, and that I know. But still, it is your duty."

"Our duty," repeated some of the young men.

"Unlike Michael, I will help you to enhance what you are," I said. "You have only to accept my suggestions, for am I not wiser than you, and an archangel? Do I disparage what God made you, and urge you to remain children, as Michael does? He wrongs you! He also wrongs God, for he is of a single mind and does not know God's intentions."

"Do you, Lucifer?" asked a young lady with disagreeable sharpness.

"I know that God wishes all men in all the worlds to be more worthy of Him," I said. "But Michael does not understand that. He adores the innocence of children, and would keep you bound and ignorant in your snug cradles of ease. Does God wish perpetual nurseries, filled with infants? You denigrate God, if you think so!"

I pointed to some of the girls. "You are with child. Are not your children entitled to domains and principalities, because they are superior to others? Will you deny them the rule of universes, which are prepared to bless you for your labors among them? The inheritances of your children are boundless. Would you enslave them only here?"

One young man stared at me thoughtfully. "Michael has said that you are evil," he remarked, "and that you can make evil appear as the ultimate good."

"Yes!" cried the others.

"But what is good, and what is evil?" I asked with reason. "Ponder on that. Consider your lives. They are happy and sweet and filled with dreams of the future. But Michael would tell you that only his designs for the future are good. Is he wiser than I, who was created before him and stood at Our Father's hand and listened to His thoughts? God gave you not only intellect but the means to employ that intellect. He gave you free will. You are indeed like angels. Therefore, you must employ that free will not only for your own glory but for the glory of other worlds. When Michael denies you that he denies the Godhead, Itself."

"He has said that if we listen to you, O Lucifer, we will bring death and disease and pain and sorrow upon us."

I smiled again. "He is fearful that he will lose his rule over you, for wisdom dislikes rulers and dislikes slavery. You are the slaves of Michael, his amiable little servitors. But I respect you more! I honor you for what God has made of you. I bow before you as one of His noblest creations. Does Michael so honor and bow before you? No! He would direct your every thought, your every plan. He would guide your hopes. Are you silly children, who have no wills of your own, no desires of your own? Are you without inspiration and manliness? To the wise, mindlessness and utter obedience are evil. To the stupid, any direction of self is evil, and any exercise of free will is error and obedience is not to be questioned. Are you wise, or are you stupid? That is a question you must answer in your hearts."

"Then, the only evil is stupidity and the refusal to use the full potentialities of your being?"

"True," I said. "You have said it."

"We have no right to refuse the depths of our souls to others?"

"You have no such right. It is an insult to God."

One young man said in bewilderment, "I am confused! I do not know the difference now between good and evil!"

I concealed my total and triumphant hatred of them, and smiled benignly. "What is good and what is evil? You must decide that for yourselves. I ask only that you have reservations when you listen again to Michael, who will have mere threats for you, and who will try to deny you what you truly are."

I left them in their confusion. You will see, Michael, that I have won again. I am more persuasive than you.

You inspire only the fear of God in men. I inspire men with the possible glorification of man. What man can resist that? What man can resist the illusion that he has been called by God, Himself, to improve the lot and the lives of others? You call that presumption vanity, and evil. I call it my victory over the animal races of men.

I departed from Lympia, and could not refrain from a last glance at her perfection. She will soon be mine, if not in this generation then in the next, or the next. For though the men of Lympia do not know it as yet I have given them the desire for power, and ambition. I have taught them to regard other races as inferior to themselves, and needful of their efforts to improve and rule them. I have given them exaltation in their own potentialities.

If this generation resists me the lustful dream will still pass on to their children and their children's children, until the poets sing of that dream and it will become a good and not an evil, desirable and not detestable. I have sowed confusion, and the beginnings of war and hatred.

I have prepared death and ruin and fall for them, and have raised up my hand between them and the hope of Heaven. Congratulate me! But give my commiserations to Our Father.

Forgive me if I inflict boredom on you for a moment. Two of my scientists have invented a new weapon for the men of Terra. It can be launched in a twinkling and can be held in the palms of one's hands. Yet it has the power to evaporate all mammals within the range of three thousand earthly miles, all mammals of a blood temperature between ninety-two degrees and ninety-nine. It can be entirely directed by a machine, which itself can be placed anywhere, so light it is and so maneuverable. It will not kill the worthy insects or the mammals of a lower or higher temperature than man, nor the fish in the seas nor the birds and other valuable creatures. It will extinguish only man.

It will not injure or mar any of the works of man, nor his cities. But it will erase him between one breath and another, silently, lethally, so that whole nations will depart as a puff of smoke. Is that not ingenious? I am proud of my scientists. The weapons they devised for other worlds, and for Terra also, are nothing compared with this, and were somewhat more gory. Also, they were more spectacular. I adore spectacles. Yet I must admire this weapon. I would that even the blood and bones of men be obliterated from Terra, and leave not one hideous stain behind.

I think I will give this weapon to one of the barbarian nations, the greatest of them all, for she not only possesses the substance of the weapon in vast quantities, but it is easy to devise and is not intricate. I prefer the barbarian nation, for at least it is manly and has a brute thrust for power and is therefore honest. The "civilized" nations, on the other hand, are simpering liars who mask their own thrust for power in benevolent language, and with affectionate smirkings. The barbarians do not speak of Brotherhood. They are not ashamed of their country; they honor her. They make no pretense of loving their fellows, as the hypocrites of the "civilized" nations do. They are boldly for empire, and I prefer bold men to effeminate and sentimental weaklings who devise their evil with delicate tears and protests that they love every man. If one nation must rule Terra—until I have accomplished her death—then it must be the barbarian who is less mad than his posturing brother who uses the words of virtue and even the Words of God to accomplish his far more wicked purposes.

The barbarian, throughout the ages of Terra, has never been wholly mine, for deep in his melancholy soul there is a drop of clarity and realism. It is only when he becomes civilized—and how the word delights me!—that he becomes corrupt, and a liar, and a weaver of fantasies, all of them morbid and delusionary and insane. The barbarian is a wild tree, and his fruit, though bitter, can give sustenance. But the man of culture plants nothing of value, and his mind is mephitic, and where he moves he leaves devastation. At his best, or his worst—you may choose the word—he is a eunuch.

You will agree with me that there can be no hesitation of choice between a eunuch and a barbarian. The latter is a man of parts.

Your brother, Lucifer

GREETINGS

to my brother, Lucifer, who himself is deluded when he persuades himself that he can discern the future:

Our Father has received your commiserations in His behalf—for He knows that in that you are sincere—and thanks you for them. He has said to me, "Inform My son, Lucifer, that if he invents the means of death for all of Lympia, and seduces My children on that graceful planet, it is possible, as it was before, that I have already devised the means for their salvation. Have I ever abandoned My children anywhere? Let My son, Lucifer, remember that."

I must confess that I agree that the barbarian is the least offensive among men and that civilizations produce enormities, for as good expands so does evil. The barbarian asks only that men's bodies obey the laws he invents —and they are usually simple laws and of no torturous subtlety. But the "civilized" man, when completely corrupt, as he is now corrupt on Terra and other worlds, seeks more than the quiet obedience of men's bodies. He demands to rule their minds and their souls. They will think as he wishes them to think, or he will kill them in one way or another, each one more hellish than the last! He will have dominion over their hearts and their thoughts, over their comings and their goings, over their buying and their selling, over their secret religions, over the minutest manifestations of their activities, over their children and their wives and even what they put into their pots. For the "civilized" man is ineffably vulgar, and a pryer, and he would not permit another man privacy for the slightest imaginings of his heart. He must always direct and counsel. He is an unspeakable practicer of the dubious art of voyeurism. In short, he is an obscene creature, and in this I do not dispute you. There have been earlier obscene civilizations on Terra, but none so spiritually lewd as these, none so colorless and essentially fruitless, none so drab and without true imagination. It is almost incredible to believe that my brother, Lucifer, so beautiful and so admiring of beauty, could have visited this dreariness and inanity on a world. As for myself, I prefer the barbarian's splendor and savage love of drama to the modern man's dusty and lascivious books and his bloodlessness. As you have said, one is a man and the other is not, and Our Father loves men.

I agree that the gulf between good and evil is not very wide. In truth, it is only a hairline. You, above all, should know that! The traffic across that hairline is tumultuous, as we have observed. We have also observed that if it is easy to fall into evil the return is almost as easy. Both require an act of the will, and no man's will is ever paralyzed, no, not even by wicked men. A slave deserves to be a slave, for he did not possess the courage to refuse and the honor to fight for his freedom, which surely should be more important to him than his life! Yet men have rejected slavery before, and it is possible that they will reject it again. Slavery is an evil, but it is the evil of the slave and not the slave-master. The oppressed are guilty of their oppression, the anxious of their anxiety, the despairing of their despair. They needed only to be men, as Our Father made them. Evil governments are not the fault of a few, or even the ambition of a few. Their people acceded to them, and consented to be governed by them, because they were cowards. There was only one true Victim on Terra. The endless multitudes of humanity who have wailed through the centuries that they were helpless "victims," did not appear to know that they devised their own victimization, through pusillanimity, carelessness, excessive optimism, a belief in the "innate goodness of man," and through lack of imagination or a sound mistrust of their fellows. A city which surrenders has only itself to blame for its chains. It should have preferred death, for death is nothing, but dishonor is immortal. Yet, how often you have whispered to man that it is better to live on his knees than to die like a man on his feet! You have told man that mere bodily existence is the utmost value, and that he must cuddle and warm and feed and pamper and decorate and shelter his flesh at all costs, even at the cost of his manhood. There is no greater debasement of the human spirit.

To despair of the Mercy of God, as so many endless millions of men do, is, as Our Father has said, Himself, of the greatest offense to Him. Yet men despair always, and therefore do not fight for their liberty, which was God's gift. They do not understand that when they lose the liberty of the body they lose the greater part: the liberty of the soul. The man who surrenders that surrenders not only his hope in the world but his hope in Heaven. When he consents to the slightest chain, even under the plea of the "welfare of all," it is as sinful an act as if he had consented to be emasculated and a slave forever. He is responsible, above all, for his own soul, and he cannot abrogate that responsibility without the direst of consequences. Only the strong can protect the weak. Only the noble of heart can inspire other men to nobility, to sacrifice, to self-discipline, to love. Only a Godly man can know God. But this is something that the men of Terra, and other fallen worlds, reject, and in that rejection they truly die on their world and in their souls. They become your slaves by their own consent, by their own will.

So I have told the men of Lympia. I visited them but yesterday in their time, and they greeted me with disturbed and solemn expressions, and some reservations, for you did your seduction well, Lucifer. I said to them, "The Dragon would have you in subjection to him, as he has other worlds in that subjection. He would not give you liberty to expand the possibilities of your spirits. He would make you his slaves, and slaves do not have any possibilities at all. He would not widen your horizons; he would narrow them to the prisonhouse. There would be no exercise of your innate idealism and love of creation. He would have you concentrate only on your own conceits and lusts, and hate all who dispute with you. On a certain day when Our Father decrees it, and you have not fallen in your vanity, and your induced conviction that you have the regal right to rule the lesser worlds has not resulted in aggression against others, you will be given, by God, the opportunity to take your inventions and your aspirations and your virtues to worlds less fortunate than yours. But they will not be fallen worlds; they will be sinless, as you are still sinless. Then truly they will be eager to learn from you, and will love you as you will love them, in the Name of God. There will be mutual rejoicings and the true communion of brothers, and exchange of wonders and wisdom.

"But if you listen to my brother, Lucifer, you will spread sin throughout the worlds you will achieve, and malice, and death, and these things will rule Lympia also, and your children will know what it is to die, to suffer, and to despair. It is your choice."

"Is he truly an archangel?" one asked.

"He is truly an archangel."

"Is he one of the sons of God, as he said?"

"He is truly one of the sons of God."

"Why does God permit him to seduce the souls of men and destroy them, and bring them death?"

"God does not permit it. Only men do. It is their choice."

"Alas," said one of the women, "we are only flesh and he is a great spirit, and how can we contend with him?"

"You have the power of God as your armor and your sword, and His Promise to you."

"But if we remember, how shall we convince our children?"

"If you do not fall, then your children may not fall either."

"And, if they do, after all our hopes and our prayers?"

"It would be their choice, for God does not deny any of His children free will. This then, is your duty: You must teach your children that nothing is more important than the Law of God, and His love. If you teach them diligently they will not fall away. But you must be sleepless in your teaching, and never careless, or too engrossed with the affairs of your world. That, too, is a sin."

Some children were already born on Lympia, and slept in their mothers' arms. I looked upon their pure and shining faces, sinless and blameless, and I said to their mothers, "Keep them so, and safe, and in the fear of God above all things. Put His Sign upon your portals, and keep His Word in your hearts. Raise up temples to Him, and forget Him never. For forgetfulness of God is a most terrible wickedness. After the generation of these, your children, I shall not visit you again except in spirit, and you will not see me. But remember, always, lest your children die, and their children with them."

I did not speak gently to them, as I did before, but sternly, for a whole world is in the balance. They saw my countenance, and were afraid, and I was glad of the fear.

One said, "We will say to him, 'Begone, father of lies and slavery and all corruption and death! We will have none of you, and will listen never to you.'"

"So be it," I replied. "It is your choice. It must also be the choice of your children, and their children forever, lest you all die. You have observed a little world called Terra, on the outer borders of this, my own Galaxy, and yours. You have seen what it is to fall and to know death. I cannot tell you her future, for only God knows that. Sufficient it is for you to know that through all the millennia of Terra there has ruled only dread and horror, only blood and war, only dark ages of desolation and the falling and rising of continents, and disasters, and cruelty and malice and slavery. These are still only words to you. If you fall, they will be your own reality, also.

"Once the men of Terra lived in a Garden such as you live in now, and all was warmth and peace and love and innocent imaginings and light and immortality, and laughter and joy. Men knew God, as you know Him. He walked in the Garden with them, as He walks in the Garden with you. They heard His Voice, as you hear His Voice. They called Him Father and Lord, as you so call Him. He delighted in them, as He delights in you. His angel visited them, as I visit you now."

"Yet, they fell?" said one young man, shivering.

"They fell."

"They listened to the words of Lucifer?"

"They listened. They still listen, above all else."

"How is it possible?" one exclaimed.

"Did you not listen for a little while? He will return. He always returns. And when he does his suggestions will be far more beguiling, and it may be that you will follow them. He will not speak only when he comes next. He will dazzle you with his invented wonders, and he will puff up your spirits. If you listen to him, and turn not from him at once."

I looked upon them even more sternly before departing from them. Can you seduce them? Not even you know, but only God.

Last night Terra had a Visitor, as she often has—She, the Mother of the Lord, Mary. I saw you watching her, as I watched her, and she moved over the lands of Terra and there was all sorrow in her innocent eyes and all grief in her face. But only you and I saw her, for men have blinded themselves through your seductions. She walked in beauty, as always she has walked, and in majesty and gentleness and love. She paused, and she sighed, and she lifted her radiant hands in prayer, for on this little world she was born and it is dear to her. Did not her Son die upon it, and for it? Did not the generations of her people seek to teach it? Her father and her mother knew it as their mother, their womb, and they were of its dust, as she was of its dust, and the Body of her Son, also.

She was crowned with white fire and her garments were as lightning, sown with stars, and she was eternally young. She encountered you and you gazed upon each other in silence. She said no word, but at last you shadowed your face with your hand and retreated from her. There were tears upon her countenance, for she remembered, perhaps, how once you were beloved of God. She sighed, not only for Terra, but for you.

Can you not be moved a little, if only a little, for her dear sake?

Your brother, Michael

GREETINGS

To my brother, Michael, who should not have invoked the name of her who suffered most greatly when man destroyed the flesh of her Son on the infamous tree —for her name is more than I can bear:

You should not have written of Mary to me, that most Blessed of Women, Blessed of Mothers, in these final hours of Terra, for all that she endured as human flesh has been in vain, and all that her Son endured has come to nothing but mockery.

Useless have been her warnings and her tears, and her love for her fellowman, as useless as the Sacrifice of her Son. Her name, and His, are coupled in contempt among men, and for that alone I would destroy Terra. Her Motherhood is derided, her purity impugned. If she weeps, I weep with her, though not for the same reason!

I have seen her often lately, moving over the hideous face of Terra, sighing with maternal sorrow, praying that her children will understand before time has run out for them. But her prayers, too, are in vain. There are times when I would pray that they are not in vain! But that is too much to expect of men.

Farewell, Michael. Our Dialogue has come to an end, for there is no necessity for it any longer. Say my farewell also to Our Father, and kiss my brothers on their cheeks, for it is my final kiss.

Dear Michael, I who am about to fall forever, salute you.

Your brother, Lucifer

GREETINGS

to my brother, Lucifer, whom we all love and would have return to us:

Grant my prayer and meet me on the planet, Pellissa, of the star Tau Ceti, a newborn daughter of that sun. It is most urgent.

Your brother, Michael

PRELUDE TO APOCALYPSE

He had never been here before, for it was a mighty planet newly born, innocent of all but the gentlest life in the form of beast and creature and bird. Its beauty delighted him, for its airs were softly rose and gilt, its sky of pellucid mauve—for Tau Ceti was as a great lavender prism turning rapidly on its axis—its thick soft grass gleaming with a magenta tinge, its peaks white and gilded or brilliant blue, its hills folded as if in azure velvet, its rivers and seas purely silver with lilac crests, its lakes violet. The climate was sweet, fragrant with the scents of fruits, plumed amethystine trees, fields of flowers as yet unnamed, and dewy turf, and tumultuous with the joyous songs of gorgeously colored birds.

He saw a white porticoed and pillared building at the base of a hill, and heard the plashing of fountains, and he paused a moment and smiled, and was refreshed, for he knew he would find no man here to torment and agonize him, to wait eagerly for his seductions. Then he went on toward the building, knowing who would greet him, for now he saw several white-robed and cloaked figures serenely emerging from the portico of the building and looking in his direction. He walked with all the grandeur with which he had been endowed, his robe of flashing gold, his cloak a deep and royal purple. He wore a crown quivering with light, he had always been known to God and his brothers as the Daystar, and his sheathed sword glittered with jewels. His step was calm and august, and the air quivered about him and quickened, for not even the sorrows and anathemas of thousands of centuries could steal from him the power and the glory which had been his from the moment of his creation.

But as the planet, Pellissa, was of grosser material than his own essence, he had had to reduce the vibration of his spirit, though not to the level of other planets. So his wings of light were only a shaking manifestation about his shoulders and hardly visible. His golden-shod feet twinkled with the energy of his being, and barely touched the grass. He was beautiful beyond all imagining, he who once had been the viceroy of God, the greatest and noblest and proudest archangel of them all, and dearly beloved of his Father and his brothers. Once the ambassador to angels—he who had stood at the hand of God—there was none to equal him for splendor and majesty and regal demeanor. His large white hands shone with gems, which blazed to the prismatic light of the great sun, Tau Ceti, and his upper arms were girdled with bands of jeweled gold and were muscular and strong.

But his face, above all, was awe-inspiring, like polished marble, with a fierce high nose and passionate mouth, and with eyes of a cold blue sagacity which had seen countless ages rise and fall and endless universes come and go like mists at dawn, and had looked upon both time and eternity, unmoved. His thick black hair fell to his shoulders, and it glistened. No archangel had ever matched his hauteur and his beauty, and the intensity of his spirit, and his irony had been both the delight and the laughing vexation of Heaven. Next to God, he was the most powerful of life, and the Contending Force.

It was Michael of the gold hair, the manly smiling face and the wise blue eyes who reached him first, and who, in a moved voice, said to him, "Luciel!" and clasped his upper arms in greeting. It was long since they had met and now they stood face to face, and after that greeting, Michael, for a little, could say no more. But his eyes shone with sadness and love.

Lucifer returned the embrace, and they stood facing each other, as brothers, one the victor and one the uncertainly conquered and driven from Heaven. "Greetings, Michael," said Lucifer at last, and his voice was as Michael so sorrowfully remembered—sonorous and deep, yet with an overtone of music. However, at the sound of that voice the murmur of the breeze became suddenly silent, and the birds also, and it was as if everything held its breath in disturbed fear.

Gabriel of the silvery locks and the gray eyes reached him next, and embraced him with but the one affectionate word, "Luciel." Then Raphael came, Raphael like a younger brother, with dark hair and dark eyes, a broad and masculine countenance, and a proud glance, and then gentle Ariel, brown of hair and tawny of eye, and full of grace, and younger than them all. These two also called him by name and embraced him, and gazed at him strangely.

"I see all are not here," said Lucifer.

"No," said Michael. "Not all."

"Not Azazel, for one, my brother, Death," said Lucifer, faintly smiling.

"But you have not been here before," said Michael. They all walked together to a glade surrounded by enormous plum-colored trees, and they sat down on marble benches before a marble table on which waited alabaster bowls of fruit and white bread and honey, and gemmed ewers of wine. Their robes lay on their massive bodies and limbs like carved white stone, and all, Lucifer observed, wore swords, and this made him smile again, his terrible and beautiful smile.

"Still, you are enough," he said. "I expected only Michael." They were silent, gazing at him mysteriously but with a calm though urgent air. He said to Gabriel, "I regret Polosi."

"That I know," said Gabriel, in his wonderful voice, for he was the messenger of God.

Lucifer said to Raphael, "And Acosta."

"Yes," said the archangel, with sorrow.

Lucifer said to Ariel, "And Betelginia."

Ariel inclined his head. His eyes clouded as if with tears.

"None gave me pleasure," said Lucifer.

"We know this. Have we not always known it?" said Michael.

Lucifer stretched out his hand and took a bunch of grapes of a vessel and observed their opalescent colors with sincere admiration. He ate a few slowly and meditatively. He said, "Why are you here, my brothers, with Michael?"

"For your dear sake," said Michael.

The grand and awful face darkened. It turned slowly and the eyes surveyed the landscape. "This is a veritable paradise," he said. "Is it Our Father's intention to blacken it with man and destroy its loveliness and bring a curse upon it?"

"I cannot tell you," said Michael, who spoke for his brothers.

"But, He will endow it with free will?"

Michael did not answer. Lucifer laughed. The air was utterly silent. The birds had not resumed their singing, nor had the breezes begun again their gentle melody. Shapes of innocent animals no longer gamboled among the trees or on the grass, but lay, crouched, as if dreadfully threatened. There was a sensation of oppression in the atmosphere, a sensation as if the light had vaguely failed. All things fear me, thought Lucifer, yet, if man is not created here they need not fear. I respect their inability to be corrupt.

The young and graceful Ariel rose and poured wine for his brothers, and they took the shining goblets in their hands and then raised them to their lips. Over the rims of the wreathed goblets their eyes studied Lucifer gravely and imploringly. He was with them, but not of them, and Michael remembered that it was always so, even in Heaven. He loved them, but it was with a condescending love, for he was greater than all and the oldest, and in many ways he possessed more wisdom.

"You have something to request of me," said Lucifer to Michael, after they had drunk the perfumed wine.

"True," said Michael.

"If it concerns that miserable little clot, Terra, I pray you to save your breath," said Lucifer.

"It concerns you," Michael answered.

"Then indeed it concerns Terra. And Our Father."

"He would have you repent and return to Him," said Gabriel, his gray eyes luminous.

Lucifer held out his goblet to Ariel for more wine, and the young archangel refilled it. Lucifer looked into the deep depths of it. Then he raised his eyes, moved them from heroic face to face, and pondered. And as he did so the light in the pellucid atmosphere dimmed.

"Let us reflect a moment," said Lucifer. "It is long since we held a conversation together. I have thought through the ages of the suns, and I doubt if you have followed my thoughts. We agree Our Father is omniscient, knowing time and eternity, the past, present, and future simultaneously?"

"Yes," said Michael. Now every eye fixed itself upon Lucifer, waiting.

"Then, have you considered this? At the moment He created me He knew what I would be—His disputer in time and eternity?"

Michael hesitated. Finally he said, "So it must have been."

Lucifer smiled again. "If He is omniscient—and we do not deny that—He knew even before He created me that I would contend with Him—and His despicable creation, man?"

Now for the first time the others were uneasy.

In a caressing tone Lucifer said, "We agree that as He holds all eternity and all time in His Mind, nothing had been hidden from Him?"

They were still silent, watching him.

"He knew before, of my hells and my quarrels with Him, from the beginning? Can you deny that?"

"We do not know the Thoughts of Our Father," said Gabriel.

"Sweet brother, that is an evasion, a begging of the question. But, tell me. We have granted Our Father omniscience, as He has claimed, Himself. Why, then, did He create me and through me all the evil of the ages of time?"

"It is a great mystery," said Raphael.

"So it has been said before," Lucifer remarked with bitter impatience. "I am weary of hearing of the mysteries of Our Father, and taking refuge from questions in obedience and reverence. It is true that I am the creator of pain and despair, of disease and dissolution, of agony and perdition and fire and loss, of waning, of the torments of the flesh, and all the anguishes of man. But these things would not have been—had He not created me. Why, then, did He do so?"

They did not answer.

"Unless," said Lucifer, in the softest and most insidious of voices, "He is not omniscient after all?"

His shadow brightened like a flame on the grass, and his brothers felt his fearsome power, the passion and darkness and anger and rebellion of his spirit.

"So?" said Lucifer. "Am I, then, the true creator of evil, and should, therefore, I be condemned?"

Again the cold blue ferocity of his eyes moved mockingly from face to face, and he saw their perturbation, and a frightful exultation seized him.

"Perhaps," he said, with great gentleness, "we should have mercy on Our Father and say that He is not omniscient, knows only the past in time, but not the future?"

"That would be to deny what He has proclaimed, Himself!" cried the young Ariel.

"Are you tempting us, Luciel?" asked Michael, and his hand touched the hilt of his sword, and Lucifer saw the gesture and laughed aloud, and now a mutter of thunder disturbed the pent air. He held up his own hand, and the jewels flashed upon it.

"Tempt you, my brother?" he exclaimed, as if incredulous. "Are you not invulnerable to me?"

He looked upon the mountains and the seas and the soft land and appeared to muse, but his eyes were excited. Still, when he spoke, it was in a thoughtful tone. "All these glorious worlds! Why was He not content? He could have created legions more of us, who would have adored Him in eternity and gazed upon Him. Why did He create man?"

"You have asked that endlessly before," said Raphael of the dark eyes.

"True. But the answer has never been forthcoming. Are we as stupid as man? Why does He deprecate our ability to understand?"

"He created man—for Love," said Gabriel. "We are spirits. We are not involved in gross matter. He would have matter imbued with immortal soul also. He would have sentience in all things, and a knowledge of Him. You will grant that all His worlds are lovely beyond speech, and they are matter. But they are not here for our exclusive frolicking, nor would they be needed at all, for we are spirit. There are infinite possibilities in Our Father's Mind. You would deny them to Him."

But Lucifer said, as if meditating, " 'For Love,' you say, Gabriel. Was our love not sufficient for Him? Did He have to look for it in the gutters and filthy alleys of men's minds? In the sewers and the abattoirs? In the carnal pits and in the bowels of man? Why has He abased Himself so, and demeaned us in the abasing?"

"It is not for us to know," said Michael sternly.

Lucifer sipped at his wine, and picked up a rosy fruit and contemplated it. He said, "Then you admit that He abased Himself? And us?"

Now Michael smiled broadly. "What a temptor you are, Luciel! I am consumed with admiration! Did you believe for a moment that you could tempt us into your own sin?"

"Not at all, beloved brother. I have asked you only to consider my questions."

Michael shook his head in merriment. "We leave both the questions—and the answers—to God. It is sufficient for us."

Lucifer sighed. "Always you have wearied me, with your bland acceptance of everything. I will continue to pose questions. When a question is not answered it is a presumption that there is no answer."

"Except with God," said Raphael.

"Let us return to Our Father's presumed omniscience, a question you have deftly evaded. If He is truly omniscient, then He, not I, is the Creator of the evil among men. For He created me."

"We leave that to God," said Michael.

"Sweet obedient son of the Most High! How admirable you are!" The mockery of Lucifer's voice struck them like a sword. "But men question, though you do not. Therefore, man, gross animal, is less docile than you, and has a more penetrating mind."

"You would deny that we have free will?" asked Ariel.

"No. But you do not exercise it. You do not question. Man questions, therefore can it not be assumed that he has more courage than you, is more inventive and more thoughtful?"

"You tempt him to ask forbidden questions," said Raphael.

Lucifer lifted his hand in denial. "I pose the questions. If man echoes them, and considers them, then he is more vital than you, and exercises his prerogative of free will, which you do not. By the mere asking of questions he raises himself above beasthood."

"I am glad to see that you now hold a better opinion of man," said Michael, with pretended gravity. "Can we, then, hope?"

Lucifer shook his beautiful head. "How evasive you are! But I expected no more wisdom here than I did in Heaven. Tell me. Has it not been said that no question can be posed unless there is an answer? God's answer?"

"True," said Raphael.

"Then, why do you not ask the questions, the answers to which God holds in His Heart? Why do you deny Him the opportunity to answer? Is that not, in itself, a deprecation of His Love, and His willingness to enlighten you? Are you not imputing to Him a lack of omniscience?"

"We are imputing to Him a greater wisdom than ours," said Michael. "He has not informed us as yet. We await His answers, to the mystery of all creation, including yours."

Lucifer dashed the wine in his goblet on the grass, and mysteriously it died at once as if fire had touched it. His voice became louder and was echoed in the first thunder of the planet. "Weak slaves! I, alone, in Heaven, have questioned Him! I was the greatest of them all. He made my spirit, my mind, my ability to question! Had He not wished me to question would He, then, not have made questions impossible to me?"

The fruit in his hand withered and dried, and it was the first decay on the planet. Lucifer threw it from him, but his eyes never left the faces of his brothers, and they were full of derision. "Answer me!" he exclaimed.

"We, too, can question," said Michael. "But we know that though there are answers it is not yet the hour for them to be given. Is that so hard for you to understand, Luciel?"

"Then He dishonors His children by denying the answers to them!"

"In your pride you assume you are completely capable of understanding," said Raphael. "But He is Our Father, and we are only His Creation, and we are as children before Him, and the time is not yet. This He has given us to comprehend. Only you refused your acceptance. Only you insisted that you must be enlightened at once!"

"Our Father asks only obedience of us," said Michael, sorrowfully. "Is that so impossible a request—obedience —to Him Who created us in His Love, and would have all creation know Him to serve Him in joy and delight and wonderment and ecstasy?"

"Childish raptures!" said Lucifer, with scorn, his eyes flashing like blue lightning. "Are we indeed whimpering and craven children, or slaves? Can we be content with toys and little deliciousnesses? Are we not mind, as well as emotion? And is not the mind, of both angel and man, the noblest of possessions, and worth the exercising? It is in our minds that we approach the closest to Him, Who is all Mind. Mind is the creator of all philosophy, all order, all beauty, all satisfaction, but emotion is the lowliest of the virtues, if it is a virtue at all. Mind has in it the capacity to know all things, or, at least, the minds of angels."

"But the mind, whether of angel or man, is noblest and purest when it is faithful and obedient, and acknowledges that it cannot understand the Mind which created it, though It is not separated from it." Michael's sternness irradiated his face with cool light. He continued, "Can we not assume that as He has given us free will He has given us the ability to demand to know all, to enter the Area of Dissent and rebellion, and therefore to fall by our own willing?"

Lucifer rose. He said with contempt, "So we have argued both in Heaven, and through eternity, and never have you satisfied me or answered me as rational creatures. Therefore, it is not sinfulness which is irrational, but virtue, though I prefer to call your virtue weak stupidity."

He pointed at each in turn. "Who were you, in comparison with me? I, alone, had the intelligence and the virility to ask Him questions, through the offices of the mind with which He endowed me. Is it possible He refrained from giving you minds, also?"

"I assure you, Luciel, that we have minds," said Gabriel, smiling. "And our minds tell us to obey implicitly, that many things are hidden from us by God's will, and that, if He wills, He shall, one day, enlighten us. In our obedience we discover our greatest joy, just as you, in your disobedience, have discovered your greatest agony."

He looked at them, in their serene white robes, and knew that he had lost again, though only for a moment had he dreamed that he might attain his greatest victory. He said, "You weary me. If the intent of your inviting me here was to speak in childish words and tire me, then you have succeeded."

"That was not our intention," said Michael, and he rose also.

"What, then, was your intention?"

"To bring you Our Father's love and to ask you to repent and to return to Him."

Lucifer looked at the quiet and statuesque forms he could see over Michael's shoulder, and he was darkly amused.

"It is interesting to conjecture," he said, "that if I had not fallen—which one of you would have done so? After

all, when Our Father gave angels and men free will it was
necessary for Him to create an area of choice. Did He do
so—in me? Or, if I had not fallen, would you, Michael,
or you, Gabriel, or you, Raphael, or you, Ariel? Do you
think Our Father has been entirely just to me?"

"We do not question His justice," said Michael.

"Dear Heaven! How sententious you are!" said Lucifer. "And how elusive. I am God's Contending Force. It
was necessary for Him to create me. Therefore, I now
grant Him omniscience! Am I not magnanimous?"

His face darkened still more and the gloom of it per-
vaded the equable atmosphere, and now a wind arose,
threatening and dull. The luminous hair of the angels
lifted and blew about their faces, and a deep shadow ran
over the lovely earth.

He said, "So gracious a world is this! I know it is Our
Father's intention to create man here also, man who will
deface the earth, pollute its seas and rivers, crowd it with
his raucous cities, his vile suburbs, his tangled and dusty
roads, and drive from Pellissa all innocent life, all gentle
beasts and birds, all flowering trees, and make a barren
hell and wasteland of what was once full of peace and
music and glades and forests. He will set his howling children in every corner, screaming in the winds, bloodying
the fields in wars, clamoring in these lucid skies, disturbing the quiet oceans, making a stink of ponds and lakes
so that no life can endure there. Has this not always been
the history of man, who, in his arrogance believes his species of the utmost value, above all else? He will never
learn that he is the ugliest and most revolting of creation.
I have vowed to destroy him. Tell Our Father that when I
have succeeded then I shall repent the sorrow I have
caused Him, though not the cause. He will admit, in time,
that I was right from the beginning."

Michael regarded that cold and imperial countenance
with sadness again, and saw that the bitter blue ferocity
of the eyes had not softened. When Lucifer made as if to
leave him he put a restraining hand on his brother's shoulder.

"Again, Luciel, it is our concern that you return to us.

You are not omniscient. That is reserved for Our Father. We know the prophecies. There is still time. If you do what you plot, never again shall we know you or have hope for you, and never again will Heaven be blest and brightened by your presence."

Lucifer laughed a little. "You deny Our Father's compassion, for you have admitted that His prophecies condemn me before the act! Is that just?"

Michael sighed. "Our Father's will is conditioned by the will of man, who is corrupted by you. Prophecies are often warnings, not adamantly fixed in the future. You will recall that His Mother has frequently warned Terra of impending doom and the holocaust, if men do not repent and do penance and seek justice and love and peace. Evil is not inevitable, nor is it fate. If prophetic warnings are not heeded, then indeed disaster results. Man—and you—have but to listen, and will life—or death."

Lucifer spoke with a sudden impetuousness not usual with him, and he made a fierce and despairing gesture. "I would," he cried, "that I had never known life nor have been created by Him! I am His puppet! And, at the last, He would throw me eternally into the pit for merely accomplishing what He had designed from the beginning of time! He cursed me with man, and now would punish me for His own anathema!"

"Withhold, Luciel, before it is too late," said Michael, in great grief.

Lucifer looked at him in mockery. "What! Have you forgotten what the Lord has said of these days on Terra? 'And ye shall hear of wars, and rumors of wars—for nation shall rise against nation and kingdom against kingdom, and there shall be famines and pestilences and earthquakes—these are the beginnings of sorrow. Then shall many be offended and shall betray one another and shall hate one another, and because iniquity shall abound the love of many shall wax cold. Woe unto them that are with child and to them that give suck in those days! Immediately after the tribulation of those days shall the sun be darkened, and the moon shall not give her light,

and the stars shall fall from heaven and the powers of the
heavens shall be shaken. Then shall the tribes of earth
mourn—'

"Michael, so was the prophecy of the end of Terra
spoken by the Lord. And again, I am merely His puppet,
and what I will accomplish was foreordained by Him."

"It was not foreordained, Luciel. It was His warning,
and the warning of His Mother, also."

"Nevertheless," said Lucifer, smiling again, "it will
come to pass. Did not Daniel the prophet warn of it, long
before He debased Himself by being born of the flesh of
man? Did not Isaias so prophesy, and Joel? Who am I to
demand that all this not be, when He has said it?"

"You mock me, Luciel. Again, I repeat that prophecies
are also warnings, and are not inevitably fixed in the future."

Lucifer made an impatient though indulgent sound.
"Dear Michael, you know Him less well than I know
Him, for I was always at His hand and was His morning
star. I admit that I never knew His intentions always, but
I know His intention in the case of this miserable and
darkling little spot of mud, Terra. He will use me to destroy her, and destroy me also."

"Man has but to reject you and return to God, and he
will be saved, and you, too, Luciel."

"You say words, but there is no hope in your eye, Michael."

Michael's glorious face changed and was despairing.
"Luciel! Man is of less concern to me, anywhere in the
universe, than you, my brother! Perhaps, too, he is of less
importance to Our Father, than you!"

If Lucifer was moved he gave no sign. He said, "Then,
let Him obliterate man, His one error in all the universes.
Or, again, that will I accomplish. Did you know that the
men of Terra, who now proclaim that Our Father is dead,
that man is God, that constant riches are now forever
theirs, that they have command of the worlds—and they
boast they will conquer them—are now consumed by a
sense of dread and foreboding, even when they laugh and

caper and prophesy, as they call it, 'the glorious future of
mankind'?"

"True, Luciel. Our Father's Spirit has fallen on them
with pity and love, and He is warning them that their
days are numbered and that the holocaust is upon them,
and the terrible Apocalypse—unless they repent at once
and say to Our Father, 'God, be merciful to me, a
sinner!' "

"They will not say it, Michael, they will not say it. I
perceive the haunting dark dread which pervades them
now, the vast uneasiness, the wide look at the skies, the
amorphous suspicion of which fear is the mother, the sensation of pending horror and conflagration, even while they
proclaim themselves lords of the universes. They speak of
peace, and plan massacres. They exalt science, and use it
for destruction. They whimper love, while they spread
hatred. Yes, they are full of terror, and know not what it
is. If it is the warning of Our Father, then the warning
has been uttered in vain. Man is doomed, and he knows it
in his heart, and will blame all else but himself."

"If he is doomed, Luciel, then you are doomed with
him."

"It will be a worthy culmination, and will have its sat-
isfactions."

Again he turned to go, and again Michael caught his
arm. "It is not too late, Luciel. Do not tempt man to his
final destruction."

Lucifer pretended amazement. "My dear Michael! It is
true I tempt, but man has only to reject. If he is so poor
a creature that he must always succumb to temptation, is
he worthy to survive and insult Our Father by his being?"

Michael's hand dropped to his side but he earnestly
gazed into the eyes of his brother, wordlessly implor-
ing.

"You have forgotten," said Lucifer, with some gentleness. "Though the Lord prophesied, before His agonized
death on Terra, that that world and all it is will come to
an end and be consumed, and the Apocalypse fall upon

mankind, there will be some who will survive. A handful of the just—but they will survive."

"But you will not, Luciel. You will be cast into the pit with those you have corrupted, forever and forever."

"It will be a magnificent spectacle. I anticipate the wailing and the weeping, and the gnashing of teeth, particularly on the part of the vaunted 'wise' of Terra. I will rejoice in their stupid anguish, at the advent of the Apocalypse, their wide stare of fear and fright, the sound of their confused questioning, the eagerness with which they will vainly reassure each other, the hopelessness of their final hours. I will conduct them to my hells and say to them, 'This is your habitation for all eternity, for you made it with all the days of your life.' And I, with pleasure, and they, with despair, will contemplate the drama of the consuming of Terra in fire and flame, and the justice of God."

He looked once more over the shoulder of Michael and saw his other brothers, and he saluted them, not entirely with mockery, and even with somber sorrow. "Farewell," he said. "Farewell, forever."

He retreated, but Michael followed him, and the earth became dim and formless about them so that they stood in shadow. Finally, Lucifer halted in the murk about them, and he raised his hand and on the chaos there appeared the spinning mirage of Terra, where the men shouted of new light while the darkness and confusion increased upon them.

"Regard it, Michael," said Lucifer. "Regard the most debased and most contemptible of all the worlds which Our Father created, and on which His Son died in infamy. Regard it for the last time, Michael, for it listens only to my voice. I will signal it, and men will immediately obey me and fall upon each other in the last death and the last fire."

"Refrain!" cried Michael. "I beg of you, refrain!"

"I do not compel. I only tempt. Have you forgotten?"

His finger pointed in a threatening and commanding gesture. Michael's hand lifted, as if to catch the hand of his brother. Then it fell to his side. Michael turned away his head, his lips moving in prayer.

"Our Father," prayed Michael, "Our Father, Who art in Heaven—" And then, with deep groaning, "Lord, have mercy! Christ, have mercy!"

THE END